LUCRETIA ANN ON THE
OREGON TRAIL

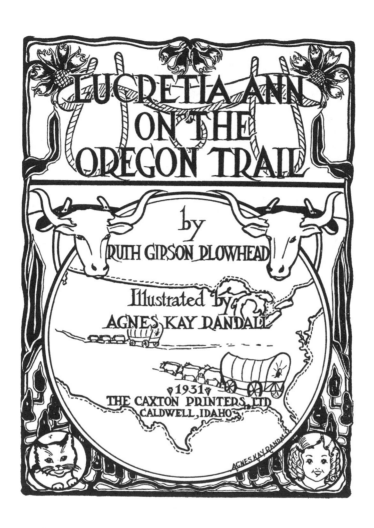

LUCRETIA ANN ON THE OREGON TRAIL

by
RUTH GIPSON PLOWHEAD

Illustrated by
AGNES KAY RANDALL

1931
THE CAXTON PRINTERS, LTD.
CALDWELL, IDAHO

1997

First Printing, August, 1931
Second Printing, July, 1933
Third Printing, May, 1939
Fourth Printing, February, 1943
Fifth Printing, September, 1946
Sixth Printing, September, 1969
Seventh Printing, October, 1993
Eighth Printing, January, 1997

ISBN 0-87004-360-9

Library of Congress Catalog Card Number 31-25267

Printed and bound in the United States of America by
The CAXTON PRINTERS, Ltd.
Caldwell, Idaho 83605
157960

To
MY DAUGHTER ELEANOR

THIS is the story of Little Miss Lucretia Ann Prence, who crossed the plains with Benjamin, tortoise-shell cat, who seemed born to trouble as the sparks fly upwards.

It tells how Little Miss Lucretia Ann:

floated down the rushing river like a huge water lily. caught the toe of her strap slipper in the picket fence and, oh, sorrowful tale! tore a jagged hole in the gay-sprigged calico apron.

stood on a high rock, with Little Friend Dimmis Greensleave, surrounded by Indians.

became a little Indian girl, wearing a buckskin tunic, weaving a basket and digging camas.

It also tells how Benjamin

went to jail.

was taken by Big Mouth.

stole the salmon and spilled the water.

broke his promise, right the day he gave it!

AND yet, in spite of all these things, and many more, Lucretia Ann and her tortoise-shell cat reached their Land O' Dreams—Idaho.

TABLE OF CONTENTS

Page

Little Miss Lucretia Ann Prence learns that she is to have an adventure 13

O Grandmother Pettigrew, let's just have corn-meal mush for supper tonight 29

The red, red apple 47

Lucretia Ann wished she were back in Grandmother Pettigrew's arbor eating early peaches and drinking raspberry shrub with cool, tinkling ice in it 63

Water! Water! Everybody come as fast as you can hurry! Water! 79

Wasn't that the jolliest kind of a birthday, anyway? 93

Indians! Indians! Run! Hide! Run! 109

There's nothing to do but go where these Indians take us 127

Look! Lucretia Ann! Look at that bad girl! Did you ever see the beat of what she's done? Look! ..145

Oh! Lucretia Ann! Would you dare? All alone in the dark? 165

The kind old man in the moon shed his softest, mellowest light upon the two tiny girls trudging along alone so bravely 181

Blow the bugle, Stephen. We must call a council 197

It wasn't a rabbit—it was Benjamin! 211

7

Has anyone seen a beautiful tortoise-shell cat walking all alone down the Oregon Trail? 223

Right where the sun set became the home of Lucretia Ann and her tortoise-shell cat, who, though born to trouble as the sparks fly upwards, had managed somehow to come safely across the Oregon Trail 241

LUCRETIA ANN ON THE OREGON TRAIL

Little Miss Lucretia Ann Prence learns that she is to have an adventure.

CHAPTER ONE

SITTING in the dining room of an old
New England farmhouse was a darling little girl
about eight years of age. Her head was garlanded
with a wreath of sunny curls; her eyes crinkled at
the corners from much laughter, while her smile
brightened like a sudden flash of sunshine. The
gay plaid dress reached almost to her ankles, and
was trimmed with crisscross bands of cherry-
colored ribbon.

Grandmother Pettigrew who loved gay laughter and gay garments and gay fun had made it as
a surprise for little Miss Lucretia Ann Prence in
spite of Mother's protests that it was hardly a
seemly Sunday gown for a proper child.

"Mother, Mother, you will make my daughter
vain. You are spoiling her," Mrs. Prence said with
trouble in her eyes. "How can her mind be upon
the Sabbath Day service and the sermon when it
is filled with all these worldly things?" she re-
proved.

Grandmother Pettigrew only laughed fondly
with her whole-souled, comfortable chuckles, and
patted her granddaughter's head.

"Lucretia Ann has far too much sense to grow
vain over a pretty dress! As well be proud over

the flowers which bloom in the garden. These bright colors were made for us to enjoy."

"Yes, Grandmother, I'm happier when I look nice, and I'm lots gooder when I'm happy. Oh, I love this gay, bright dress until I could eat it," she cried, gathering the billowing skirts at each side with her hands, and whirling about the room like a giddy little top which had been wound up so tight it could not stop spinning. Her bright curls flew harder and harder, her pink cheeks grew pinker and pinker, her skirts stood out straighter and straighter, until at last, breathless, she made a billowing "cheese" with the flouncy silk, gave a deep curtsy, and sank in a heap upon Grandmother Pettigrew's lap.

No wonder Lucretia Ann loved the new little dress. It was made of stiffest taffeta which rustled and crackled and billowed with hoops just as your small gathered skirts billow when you are standing over a heated register. There was a hand-wrought tucker and undersleeves of sheerest lace; pretty ruffled pantalettes peeped from beneath the flowing skirts, and altogether, Lucretia Ann was as dainty and sweet a maiden as you could wish to see.

It was yesterday that she had gotten the new dress. Today she was sitting prim and straight on the horse-hair sofa. Hands were stiffly folded in

the lap, and the small strap slippers hugged each other in despair. Dimples of laughter forgot to chase themselves across her face, for she had been a naughty girl and was wondering what the penalty would be.

Would Mother deny her at dinner the thick

luscious piece of custard pie, darkly dotted with nutmeg, which she liked so much?

Would she have to learn the longest of long psalms by heart?

Would she and Brother Tom have to spend a whole hour of this bubbly, sparkly day sitting on opposite sides of the gloomy parlor without speaking when they returned from church?

The trouble started when Lucretia Ann knelt with the family at prayers that blue and silver morning. Just being alive was so fine that it made you want to shout and jump for joy. Previous to the prayer, Lucretia Ann sat very quietly while her father read aloud from the great family Bible. There was a long passage about Abram's going from the land of Ur.

When Father boomed in his loud deep voice:

"Now the Lord said unto Abram, Get thee out of thy country and from thy kindred and from thy father's house unto a land which I will show thee," it seemed to Lucretia Ann that he looked very solemn, and that his voice trembled. Mother, too, looked sober and sad.

And then the family knelt in prayer. The tense feeling frightened Lucretia Ann until she felt like crying; indeed, a stray tear did roll down a shell-pink cheek. She licked it off with her little pink tongue, and smiled in astonishment to taste

16

how salty it was. She did not remember noticing that before.

A slight noise made her glance to one side, and there was Benjamin, her playful tortoise-shell cat, having a beautiful time. He was making springing leaps at the copper toes of the hired man's new shoes and clawing at the frayed hems of his work-worn trousers. The cunning, cunning thing! Lucretia Ann nudged her brother Tom, four years older, and the sight of Wills trying to be reverent and quiet and at the same time to shoo away Benjamin made Tom chuckle outright—a good healthy chuckle. Lucretia Ann laughed too, like the bubbling over of a joyful little spring. Then she put her hands over her mouth, shocked at what she had done. Both stiffened into horrified silence.

Levity at worship was never permitted, even by the gentle father. The morning's devotions over, Tom made a leap for the side porch. Lucretia Ann tried to glide unnoticed into the garden, but Father said:

"Children, keep your places. We have something to say to you."

Silence. Breathless, shamefaced silence. It was coming; the expected reproof. Father looked at Mother, and Mother gazed back at Father. Neither seemed willing to speak. Finally Father cleared his throat and said:

"You had better tell them, Mother."

"Oh," groaned the two inwardly, for Mother's punishments were always worse than Father's.

"Children," began Mrs. Prence hesitatingly, "you know that neighbors Sears, Lothrop, and Gibson went west to Idaho last year. We have heard wonderful reports of the fruitful new country which they have found."

Lucretia Ann began to breathe more freely. Was it possible that Mother had missed the giggles?

"So now," continued Mother in a halting voice, as though she somehow dreaded what she had to tell, "neighbors Greensleave, Sparrow, Tracy, and Greene are making a western pilgrimage. We plan to emigrate with them. Yesterday your father sold the farm to Uncle Jedediah. We will leave within a few weeks. Just as soon as we can pack and sell our things, and the caravan is ready."

No one spoke for a moment. The news was too breathtaking. The farm sold! A western pilgrimage! Why, up to this time, even a trip to the county seat twenty miles distant had been an event to cause days of excitement. Now Mother was calmly announcing that they were to go thousands and thousands of miles away. Out with the Indians and the buffalo! Through long miles of cactus and sagebrush desert.

Tom began to caper and shout for joy!

"Why Idaho, Father?" he asked. "I thought everyone went to Oregon. Why don't we go there? On to Oregon! On to Oregon! is all we hear. Everyone says it's such a beautiful, wonderful place."

"We really are going to Oregon, Son. All of that country was at one time called Oregon, and Idaho is a new territory which has been made from part of it. Some of our neighbors who started for Oregon stopped there. They liked the bright sunshine and rich land, and probably were tired of journeying, so they stayed. We would rather go where we have some friends, would we not?"

"Three cheers for Idaho!" shouted Tom with a

mighty caper. "Bring on my old six-shooter and bowie knife. I'll be ready for the buffalo and wolves and any old Indian who gets in my way. I'll scalp him fast enough!"

"Hush, Son. What a terrible thing to say. Indians have their homes and families as we do," shuddered Mother. "We are seeking a peaceful home, not warfare."

Stephen, sixteen-year-old son, was already in the secret. His determination to go with the caravan, whether his parents went or not, was the final straw which decided this important step.

Still little Lucretia Ann did not move. She felt almost as breathless as she had on the day when she fell in the icy pond while skating. She was trying to decide whether to be glad or sorry. She loved adventure, and for years had grown wide-eyed as the neighbors talked of western lands. Dimmis Greensleave was her dearest friend, and a trip across the desert with Dimmis—why, never in their loveliest planning had they dreamed of anything half so delightful.

Yet here were the spacious home and the farm, every inch of which she loved. And Lucretia Ann had a grandmother who lived in a little home next door. A regular storybook grandmother, the kind about whom every grandmotherless little girl dreams. She was silver haired, roly-poly, and sweet, and it was her own sunny smile and twinkling eyes which were reflected in Lucretia Ann's face. She wore lavender calicos, and rustling silver silks. There were a tortoise-shell cat and a singing kettle on her hearth, while her cellar was filled with sugar and spice and everything nice from cooky jars to apple bins. When Lucretia Ann's thoughts turned to Grandmother she cried quick as a wink:

"Will we take my grandmother with us?"

"I am afraid not," replied Father sadly. "All the others think she is too old to go at present. That is the hard part of leaving."

"Then why," asked the little girl indignantly, "should we go away and leave her when she loves us all? And what would I do without a grandmother?"

"That is what we are all wondering, Daughter," said Father sadly. "She will manage nicely without us, for she has Uncle Jed and family, Aunt Adelaide, and Uncle Peter."

"Well, that's not us, nor me," said Lucretia Ann stubbornly, for she well knew that she was the delight of her grandmother's heart, and no one could take her place. "And look, Father, look at that picture over the mantel," she exclaimed, pointing excitedly to the painting of a quaint little girl of a bygone century, "wouldn't that nice little grandmother who lived on this very farm over two hundred years ago, think we were funny people to go and leave it? Why, the pink moss rose bushes by the fence are from cuttings of the roses she planted. And Grandmother Pettigrew says that the great oak where I have my playhouse was planted by my great-great-grandmother Lucretia Ann. Why do we want to leave all these nice things?"

Lucretia Ann spoke very earnestly, and her voice was trembling.

What should they say to the troubled little girl? Brother Stephen took a hand.

"Sister," he said gently, "don't you remember how that funny little girl in the picture had eight brothers, and they all sailed to America? They intended to leave her behind, and send for her when they had a comfortable home. But the old aunt she was to stay with was cross, and she would not leave her brothers—not that funny little, spunky little girl. This was when she was fourteen. She ran away in one of her brother's cast-off suits, and paid her passage with the money they had left. Her brothers did not see her until they were miles out at sea. She left her home to go with her brothers. Do you want Stephen and Tom to go west without you?"

Lucretia Ann shook her head violently, still unable to speak.

"Well, you see," continued Stephen persuasively, "the brothers went to America to get more land, so they could all be together. And that is what we want. Of all the hundreds of acres those eight brothers had, there are only forty left in this farm. Out there we can get hundreds of acres for almost nothing if we will live on it. Father can have a big farm, and I'll have a farm, and Tom will have a farm, and maybe you'll marry a farmer and live by us, and we'll all live happy ever afterwards."

Lucretia Ann dimpled. She could not be sad long enough to resist a sly dig at Tom. So she said:

"Yes, Tommy must go and get his farm ready for Loretta Gates."

Tom hated Loretta with a deadly hatred. She was always tattling on him in school.

"Young lady, I'll show you about that," he called angrily, making a dive for his mischievous sister. In the scrimmage Benjamin jumped upon his small mistress' lap, as though to protect her from harm. He put his little paws upon her arm and purred loudly. That brought a new anxiety.

"Father," she inquired, "what about Benjamin? I am to take him, am I not?"

Father cleared his throat and looked at Mother. Mother looked at her hands.

"My, Daughter," he said, "a cat would be a terrible burden on this journey, and I am sure Grandmother would love to care for him for you. She will be lonely and will like very much, I am sure, to keep your kitten as company for Hezekiah. Grandmother loves cats."

"Well, I do too," sobbed Lucretia Ann, "and you want me to leave everyone I love; my nice grandmother and Uncle Peter, and now my darling kitty. I do not think I want to go. I would rather stay here."

"Tut! Tut! child. I cannot have tears at the beginning of the journey. If your heart is set upon your kitten I will see what we can do."

"I could fasten a cage to the back of the wagon," said Stephen.

"I will help care for Benjamin," promised Tom. "Of course Lucretia Ann must take her cat."

"O you nice brothers," beamed Lucretia Ann, her smiles returning. She placed Benjamin on the floor, stood him on his hind feet, and ducked his yellow head until he made a series of bows.

"Say 'thank you' to the ladies and gentlemen for all their kindness," she chuckled, and then, grabbing his front paws, she whirled the cat

24

around the room with her skirts flying, and laughing so gleefully that Mother said:

"Hush, child, remember the day."

Then she sat down breathlessly hugging her astonished cat, and listened while many general plans for the trip were discussed. At length her father said:

"Better run over and see Grandmother Pettigrew now, Lucretia Ann, for I am sure she is feeling very sad. Cheer her up. She wants to go with us. It will soon be meeting time, and Mr. Greensleave and family are returning with us to dinner so that we may talk over our plans. You and Dimmis will have many things to say to each other. So run along and chat with Grandmother now."

O Grandmother Pettigrew, let's just have corn-meal mush for supper tonight.

CHAPTER TWO

THE soft kid strap slippers dragged slowly along the winding covered corridor which led to Grandmother Pettigrew's doll-like house next door. Generally, Lucretia Ann ran with curls a-flying, skirts a-flirting, and slippers a-tapping in her eagerness, but now she was dreading the visit. Would Grandmother be sobbing in her huge arm-chair? Would her eyes look big and sad the way they had often looked these past few weeks? At the thought several bright tears went splash! splash! on the rough boards, and the troubled granddaughter said to herself:

"My dear, sweet Grandmother Pettigrew. I know now why she has been so quiet and sober these past days. What can I say to cheer her? I think Uncle Jed and Aunt Ad are just as mean not to let her come. She loves picnics, and we would take such good care of her. She seems younger than any of us and can work so hard. Well, I will promise to write long letters, and come and visit her someday."

The child hugged Benjamin tightly, paused outside the kitchen door, and raising herself on tiptoe peered through the upper glass sash. Her tears stopped flowing, and her eyes widened like

round blue moons. She grew almost indignant.
For the little grandmother whom she had come to
comfort was laughing—such a jolly, mellow, rolling laugh as Lucretia Ann had not heard in weeks.
It was a laugh that seemed to ripple from her
double chins down to her roly-poly feet.

Lucretia Ann stretched her neck the better to
see. Yes, it was true. There stood Grandmother
Pettigrew in her starchiest lavender calico dress,
and her crispy white apron with broad strings

billowing about her like drifts of snow. Her face was a wrinkle of smiles, and soft white curls had escaped her cap and were rippling about her rosy cheeks.

"Isn't she a pretty grandmother?" thought Lucretia Ann. "I wonder why she's so happy. I don't want her to feel bad, and yet I want her to miss me when I go."

She was talking to Uncle Peter—Lucretia Ann's handsome young lawyer uncle, Grandmother's baby, who had evidently arrived late the night before from the city. Grandmother was saying, "O Peter Boy, you're so good to your mother. You've never failed me yet, and have taken such a load from my mind. Peter! Peter!" Grandmother Pettigrew gave him a monstrous hug, and then, as rising smoke seemed to threaten her buckwheat cakes, she bustled to the stove. She flipped the cakes deftly on the large iron griddle, and soon placed the golden brown pile in front of Uncle Peter.

They made Lucretia Ann hungry, and she had already eaten her breakfast. At one side of the cakes was a Toby jug filled with thick maple syrup, and a saucer of melted butter; on the other was a platter of plump sausages and a comb of amber honey. Uncle Peter leisurely placed some of the cakes on his plate, buttered and flooded them with syrup, and then said to Grandmother in his low, laughing voice:

"Bless you, Mother, why shouldn't you be the one to say what you want? Any time Peter fails to heed your wishes—"

Lucretia Ann could wait to hear no more. She threw wide open the door and fell a-sobbing in the midst of the billowing white apron, crumpling it and splashing it with tears.

"Grandmother Pettigrew," she sobbed, "I thought you would be unhappy. Don't you care, even the tiniest little bit that your own little granddaughter is going so far away? Out with the Indians, and everything. And we've got to leave Uncle Peter too."

"Care, my baby!" soothed Grandmother Pettigrew, holding Lucretia Ann in her lap. "My heart has been so heavy that I could hardly drag myself about the house." She looked at Uncle Peter, and Uncle Peter responded with a solemn wink of his right eye. "Go to it, Mother," he said, "Lucretia Ann can keep a secret just as well as you or I."

"Indeed she can," agreed Grandmother Pettigrew. "I have never known her to break a promise. And this must be a very, very special promise, Lucretia Ann. We have a secret you will love, Granddaughter. So run and dash off your tears with cool water, and then draw up your chair and eat with Uncle Peter. You can enjoy some of Grandma's cakes, can you not?"

"You make the best buckwheat cakes in the whole world. I could always eat them," smiled Lucretia Ann through her tears.

Grandmother Pettigrew took down the pink luster plate with the happy nymphs dancing in circles about it. She went to the cupboard, and hunted out a pot of blueberry jam. She buttered some cakes, with thick blueberry jam in between, and cut them in the even little dice that Lucretia Ann loved to have. Then, during the breakfast Grandmother Pettigrew and gay, gay Uncle Peter between them told her the secret. And it was just as delightful a secret as Grandmother Pettigrew had said it would be. Lucretia Ann tried to throw her arms ecstatically about Uncle Peter and Grandmother at once, and only succeeded in bumping their heads sharply together. But nobody minded when they thought of the joy of the secret.

Then Lucretia Ann dutifully ran along to church with her parents and sat primly in the hard pew, just bursting with impatience to talk it all over with Dimmis, who also sat primly across the aisle. When no one was looking they made deaf and dumb signs. When she and Dimmis finally got together how they did talk!

"What do you think Idaho will be like?" queried Dimmis.

"I don't know. Father says there are big, dry plains all covered with something they call sagebrush—that's a funny name, isn't it?" giggled Lucretia Ann. "It makes me think of turkey and dressing, doesn't it you? And there are high mountains and large rivers too."

"They say there's lots of gold there too. Wouldn't it be nice if we could find a mine?"

"Wouldn't it be wonderful? We'd buy jewels and fine dresses, and come back here and astonish everybody with our riches."

"There are Indians," shuddered Dimmis. "Tom says maybe we'll be scalped. What will you do if you see some?"

"Tom thinks he's smart. Father says the Indians are friendly. I'll smile at them. I hope we'll see lots of buffalo running over the plains. I'd like a curly robe like Uncle Jed's."

On they talked and on they planned. Sometimes they walked sedately with their arms about one another's waists; sometimes they hugged each other joyfully; and sometimes they gazed round-eyed and almost frightened at one another when they thought of the desert, and the Indians, and the parting with friends.

Those two little maids would have been doubly

round-eyed, could they have seen themselves four months from that day. For they would have seen themselves wandering down the Oregon Trail at midnight—alone on the desert! They would have heard the coyotes mournfully howling, the owls hooting, and known themselves lost, frightened, shivering at every chance noise, and all this on account of the mischievous Benjamin who was now frolicking at their feet.

    ❊   ❊   ❊   ❊   ❊

So this is the way Lucretia Ann Prence learned that she was to leave the lovely New England farm home, and become a little pioneer girl in the far West.

Breathtaking times began at once. The family's life had heretofore been calm and uneventful, and never, never, could Lucretia Ann remember such excitement. She almost seemed to be hurling through space, so many things happening all at once.

"Mother," she exclaimed one day, "we hardly have time to breathe. It seems as though a hurricane wind is driving us along like a bunch of leaves. I hope we will like the place it is taking us to."

The dignified, calm old farmhouse looked almost like a junk-shop, for the Paul Prence family

was moving out, while the Jedediah Pettigrew
family was moving in. The blue- and pink-
sprigged china, the choicest heirlooms among the
furniture, the pictures, the hand-woven linen and
the household goods were packed at once, for
Stephen and Wills, the hired man, were going
ahead with these, and other things, to the Missouri River. There, neighbors would help them
buy prairie schooners, oxen, horses, and all the
supplies necessary for the long overland journey.
In the meantime Father would be settling busi-
ness at home. In less than a jiffy those things were
gone—rolling in freight wagons toward the West.

Next, there was an auction on the broad lawn.
Lucretia Ann had thought this would be jolly fun.
All the neighbors for miles about coming to buy,
and eating a picnic lunch together. At first it *was*
fun! But she almost had to shut her eyes when she
saw Father's favorite chair, Mother's sewing table,
her own trundle bed, and many other things carried away. When the little melodeon which
looked like a baby organ, and upon which she
could play four really tunes was sold, she ran and
sought out the lilac-bush playhouse. She wondered what was making the large lump in her
throat, and the smothery feeling in her breast.
Even here there was small comfort. Her cousins
Ruth and Mary shouted:

"Lucretia Ann, do play with us! We are sorry you are going away, but we are glad of this playhouse and all these dishes and toys."

"I have to go to Grandmother's; something is the matter with my throat and I cannot swallow," she said, and she ran like the wind to the dear retreat where she and Grandmother wiped away their tears together.

But there was little time for sorrow, for there was no end of things that even an eight-year-old could do. Father, Mother, and Tom stayed on in the old home, but Lucretia Ann was Grandmother's guest. And a right royal guest she was. Grandmother Pettigrew played with her, entertained her, and told her stories. Every morning she put on her most shining table linen; she brought out her thinnest sprigged china, her solid silver, and placed her small guest at the head of the table. She allowed Lucretia Ann to pour the tea, and pour the coffee. She even let her have these things to drink, and made cambric tea and coffee without putting in nearly as much cream and hot water as Mother always did. She kept her cooky jar full of Lucretia Ann's favorite caraway cookies, and her own pockets full of anise seed, and hoarhound, and peppermint lozenges, which she reached for at unexpected moments, and placed in her small granddaughter's pink palm.

There were not many of these quiet times, however, for the whole countryside wanted to honor the departing families. There were public gatherings, and private gatherings; parties, teas, and dinners.

Almost every day polite little notes, written in exquisite copperplate hand were left at the farmhouse door requesting Mr. and Mrs. Prence, Grandmother Pettigrew, Master Thomas Prence, and Mistress Lucretia Ann Prence to be present at twelve o'clock dinner, six o'clock supper, or other farewell gathering. Wearing of the gay little plaid silk dress and lovely festive garments became a daily affair. Indeed, there was so much need for "Sunday best" garments that Grandmother Pettigrew was almost at her wits' end. For she loved to see her little maid fresh as a rose, and there were fluted tuckers, ruffled petticoats, fancy pantalettes, collars, undersleeves, and daintily ruffled aprons. Mother objected to so much freshly ironed finery, but Grandmother Pettigrew said firmly:

"Now, Daughter, do not say one word. I can rest when you are gone. Lucretia Ann is my little daughter these days, and I shall dress her as I will."

As to the good things that were prepared by those famous New England cooks! It makes one hungry even to think about them! There were roast turkeys, baked chicken, hams, and roasts; pound cake, fruit cake, sponge cake, jelly roll, and spice cakes galore; pies and tarts of many kinds, and quivering mounds of blanc mange, to say nothing of jams, jellies, and preserves. Even when Dimmis and Lucretia Ann and the other children had to wait until the second table, and were so hungry that they felt hollow clear to their very toes, they could eat and eat when their turn came, and still leave a table full of good things.

"Paul, I fear your neighbors are trying to kill

you with kindness," said Grandmother Pettigrew, after the sixth company meal in four days.

"I sometimes think myself that they are," laughed Mr. Prence. "But we will doubtless have many lean meals on the desert to make up for this feasting."

"Anyway, Grandmother Pettigrew, let us just have corn-meal mush for supper tonight," begged Lucretia Ann. "I did not think I would ever be thankful for only that, but I would be now."

Perhaps the hardest thing of all was the last day visit to the school. Lucretia Ann and Dimmis, feeling very grand and important, met at the crossroads to make a farewell visit. They skipped along the dusty road, hand in hand, dressed in their company clothes.

Lucretia Ann's sunkissed curls escaped from beneath the dear little straw-colored bonnet, poke shaped, which framed her face in a mass of tiny rosebuds and forget-me-nots. Her blue challis, trimmed with many rows of black ribbon, fell in straight folds to meet hand-embroidered pantalettes.

Dimmis was like a demure little violet, wearing a wine-colored surah silk trimmed with many tucked insets. A sober black bonnet framed her pale, small face, while her smoothly parted hair fell in long braids far below her waist.

All lessons were forgotten, and the Master declared a half hour holiday, while the children crowded about. "Write to us." "Tell us about the Indians." "Be sure to find a gold mine." "You'll be scalped." "Send us some arrow heads." "Oh, we will miss you!"

"Indeed our school will be a sorry place without you two to liven it up," said the Master.

Lucretia Ann had a party all her own. A funny party, too, for only old ladies were invited. On a set of frames in the front room was stretched the gay hollyhock quilt Lucretia Ann had pieced all by herself, sitting at Grandmother's knee an hour each day. It was lovely! All in pinks and blues and yellows and lavenders. It was to go on Lucretia Ann's bed in the new home, and to help her finish it Grandmother invited in the six women in the neighborhood who were most skilled in quilting. Each had on her starched white apron, and each brought her favorite needle. Lucretia Ann put on her starched apron, stood on a hassock, and worked too. Even a tiny girl, if she had sewed by Grandmother Pettigrew for years, could take the smallest stitches when she tried. And hadn't Lucretia Ann pieced that whole quilt, and shouldn't some of her stitches be in that cover for her very own bed?

Well, those last hurrying, scurrying weeks flew

by. The railroad trip to the Missouri River flew by. And now we see Lucretia Ann a member of a caravan which is starting to wind its way across the American desert.

The trip was a long-drawn-out picnic, or camping frolic at first. Lucretia Ann felt that of all the many delightful things which had already come into her short life, this was by far the most wonderful.

"People talk about the hardships of the trip across the desert," she confided to Dimmis. "I think I've had more fun than I ever had in my life, haven't you?"

"I have too," agreed Dimmis. "We can walk with all the other children when we want, and ride when we want, and there's something new all the time. And always someone to play with."

"I know I will remember this when I am an old, old lady, lots older than Grandmother Pettigrew. I think it's too bad she is not here to share the fun. She would like it more than anyone. Oh, look at the flowers! Let's braid some wreaths to put about the oxens' necks."

No wonder the girls were enthusiastic, for the trip started out delightfully. There were fourteen families in the train, all well provisioned and with splendid equipment. There were gentle spring rains to keep the country green, flowers were blooming, and the sun beamed warmly down upon a joking, laughing, singing band of eager caravaners. The children chose to walk much of the time, keeping pace with the plodding oxen. Lucretia Ann, with her friendliness and her jokes, was always the center of this gay group. Yet when she was tired, there was the light spring wagon drawn by Mollie and Bell, the horses, and filled with feather beds and other comforts upon which she might rest at will. At night, whenever there was wood, huge bonfires were built inside the circle of wagons which were drawn and linked together both as safety for the finest livestock, and for protection against the Indians.

This was almost the nicest time of all. Lucretia Ann sat with her head against her father's knee, and listened to the Bible reading, the storytelling, the jokes, and best of all the music. The whole party would at times join in singing old familiar songs, and Lucretia Ann thought she had never heard such lovely music. Perhaps the moon would rise, big as a washtub, and Stephen and some of the other young men would reach for their banjos. The blue eyes would grow heavy, and while the boys were singing:

> "O Susanna, don't you cry for me
> I'm off to Alabamy with my banjo on my knee."

the little girl would fall fast asleep. Her dreams were always of Grandmother Pettigrew, or of a lovely new country far away, where the skies were blue, and where flowers danced in the sunlight.

The red, red apple.

CHAPTER THREE

SEVEN the most delightful of picnics in time grows tiresome, and this was like all the rest. Could you have gazed over the prairie you would have seen a long, long string of wagons, followed by oxen, horses, cattle, and dogs plodding along the Oregon Trail. They were stirring up such clouds of dust that you might have thought the whole desert was afire when those columns rolled like smoke toward the sky.

In the front wagon at the head of the train a small girl sat beside her father. With head erect and anxious eyes she was scanning the broad swift-flowing river ahead.

"Lucretia Ann," said Mr. Prence, "hop down and see what that sign says. I cannot see from here, and there is no ferryman in sight."

Lucretia Ann jumped cheerfully from the wagon and slowly and carefully read the following words:

FERRY CLOSED FOR REPAIRS.
FORD SAFE AT THIS SPOT

"O Father," cried the little daughter, "must we ford this dreadful river? I do not like it, for it seems so wide and deep and swift."

"You will not mind it, Lucretia Ann," smiled Father. "When the river is high in the spring the ferry is necessary, but the water is low at this time of year. The people who know the river here would not say it is safe to ford, if it were not. I will see if everything is in shape so that the water will not touch it before we start across."

The little girl climbed slowly back into the high, hot seat. Save for the sudden flashing smile she gave her father, you would hardly have known Lucretia Ann for the same child who flew about the New England farmyard like a happy yellow butterfly. She looked more like a forlorn, grey desert moth. The dainty wild-rose face was parched and tanned. A limp sunbonnet covered the wondrous hair. It had not lost its curl, but was lifeless and grey under a film of dust. A plain calico dress and heavy shoes had replaced the dainty frocks and kid slippers. There were no more of the fluffy white tuckers, aprons, and pantalettes which had been Grandmother Pettigrew's great delight.

And, though still sunny, she couldn't be happy and gay like a bird, for she was always tired. Sometimes it seemed as though she were a prison-

er doomed to march, march, march; jog, jog, jog;
tramp, tramp, tramp through grey scorching
deserts. And these deserts were so filled with dust
that the travelers often gasped for breath. There
was no garden glittering with dewdrops in the
morning sun, from which you might pluck gorgeous red strawberries, raspberries, currants, or
even the sourest of gooseberries to crunch between white little teeth on a dare that you would
not pucker your face even the tiniest bit.

When Lucretia Ann thought about those things
and about Grandmother Pettigrew rocking and
singing in the grape arbor, she had to hold her
head very high to keep up her courage. And she
would give her curls a toss, and say over and over
what Grandmother Pettigrew had told her to say
when things grew hard:

"I'm a little pioneer girl. I'll be a brave one.
On to Oregon!"

Father had now returned to the wagon; everything seemed safe. Lucretia Ann clutched the
seat tightly, and gave a tiny gasp as Mollie and
Bell hesitated a moment, and then went splash!
splash! into the rippling river. Deeper and deeper
grew the water; almost to the wagon bed it came.
They were nearly across. Just a moment more—

"Oh, I'm so glad," breathed the little girl, giving a vast sigh of relief. "That was the scariest thing!"

Then it happened! Quick as a wink Mollie veered sharply downstream, and stepped into a hole; she stumbled, and the force of her fall made Bell also lose her balance. The wagon gave a tremendous lurch and little Miss Lucretia Ann Prence was hurled into the rushing river.

"Help! Help! Help!" she screamed, when she could gain her breath. "I'm going down the river. Help!"

Down, down, the stream she floated, bobbing this way and that like an immense water lily. Father could not save her; he was tangled with the lines and struggling for his own life. A shout rose from across the river; Wills, Stephen, Tom—a dozen men who had been watching from the opposite shore were out of their wagons, and plunging into the stream, thinking hopelessly how hard it would be to swim or wade over and rescue their gay little companion before she was washed away. But someone was ahead of them.

A little Quaker lady, whose husband ran the ferryboat, had been attracted by the dust of the approaching train, and had walked from her home just around the bend in the river, to watch the passing of the wagons, and perhaps glean stray bits of news from the world so far away. She had

been standing unnoticed under a huge cotton-wood tree by the bank. Quick as a wink she waded in, and the water being fairly shallow, though swift, she managed to grasp that precious bit of calico which was struggling to gain a foothold. In a moment both were safe ashore.

"Oh, my father! My father! My kitten! Our lovely things in the wagon!" the drenched child managed to sputter.

"Thy father is safe. See, child. Do not cry.

The horses have regained their foothold and are climbing the bank. Where is thy kitten?"

"He's in a cage on the back of the wagon. Oh, he *is* all right. There he is. My Benjamin! Benjamin," she cried running fast as the wagon lumbered to the shore. She released the frightened cat and cuddled him in her arms.

"We're three drowned rats, aren't we?" smiled the Quaker lady.

"We are," Lucretia Ann laughed in spite of herself. "I wanted a bath in this lovely river, but not that kind."

Steve and Mr. Greensleave had now forded the river on horseback to be sure of a shallow place. By veering a little farther upstream the rest of the wagons came safely across, and all crowded about Lucretia Ann and her rescuer.

Mother, generally so calm and unmoved, grabbed her little daughter, the Quaker lady, and Benjamin all in one armful and hugged them as she sobbed:

"How can I ever thank you, friend, for rescuing my Lucretia Ann. She might have been swept down the river and drowned before any one else could have reached her. What can I do for you? What can I say?"

The little grey lady, who introduced herself as Mrs. Norris, said:

"If thou really wishest to thank me in the nicest way I can think, thou wilt allow thy daughter to spend such part of the day with me in my cabin as thou art here drying the contents of thy wagon. Thee may know, I am often very lonely. More so than ever today, for my husband and sons have driven away for repairs for the ferry, and will not be back until late night. We live just around the bend in the river. I will gladly wash and iron the little maid's clothing, and I can find her some of mine to wear while it is drying. It will be a real favor to me if thou wilt let her come."

Such a quaint little lady she was, as grey, as calm, as sunny as the desert in which she lived. She had on a Quaker grey dress and snowy fichu, and her smoothly parted grey hair would persist in crisping into delightful waves, in spite of all her efforts to keep it smooth. Lucretia Ann was charmed with this new friend, and longed with all her heart to visit in her home. She smiled her sunniest smile when Mother told her that the train had decided to camp for the day in the grove of cottonwood trees on the riverbank. The women would do a much needed washing while the Prence family dried out the contents of their wagon. Lucretia Ann, with Benjamin in her arms, and Mrs. Norris hastened away to find dry clothing.

Oh, that gracious little desert home which met their eyes as they turned the bend in the river!

Like a fairy-tale story that tiny dwelling loomed, the foundation gay with old-fashioned posies, many of them just the kind that Grandmother Pettigrew had so much loved. Hundreds of brilliant morning-glories, climbing over the cabin, nodded an astonished good morning at seeing a sweet little girl march up the path, looking like a drowned rat. When she spied the flowers she stooped to sniff their fragrance and touch them softly with her hands.

"Why, Mrs. Norris," she cried, "here is the same spicy pink that my Grandmother Pettigrew loves better than any other flower, and you have sweet williams and hollyhocks just like hers. May I gather a leaf of the rosemary and lemon verbena for Mother to smell when we go back to the wagon?"

"As many posies as thy hands will hold. But scurry into the house and let us get rid of these dripping garments."

In a jiffy Lucretia Ann was sitting in one of Mrs. Norris' starched Quaker grey dresses, with Benjamin on a cushion at her feet smoothing his rumpled coat. She was admiring the cozy little house. It was just as lovely, just as peaceful, just as gay indoors as it was outside. A bright rag carpet, springy to the feet from much straw underneath, covered the front room floor. There was a grey couch, with bright patchwork pillows and quilt, which looked almost as bright as the flowers in the garden. A golden canary sang in a golden cage, and a golden cat purred and rubbed against Lucretia Ann's little toes, as he tried to make friends with Benjamin.

"O Mrs. Norris," exclaimed the delighted child, "I think this is the very beautifullest house I was ever in. I should like to stay in it always. It looks —well, it looks just like a home." No wonder it seemed like a beautiful haven after months on the dusty trail!

"Well, suppose thou stayest with thy kitty. I would like nothing better," smiled Mrs. Norris, and then she set about entertaining her small visitor. She knew just what to do, and should have been mother to half a dozen small girls. Lucretia Ann was allowed to help pluck the early green corn, and husk it, saving the silk for corncob babies, which she dressed later in the day. She scraped the potatoes, arranged the lettuce, and dumped the quivering red jelly into any one of the pretty dishes she chose. And, just as dear Grandmother Pettigrew had done, Mrs. Norris placed her at the head of the table, and allowed her to pour the tea, as though she had been a grown-up lady guest.

Lucretia Ann in later years often laughed about that dinner. It was such a simple meal, served on a worn red tablecloth, and yet to the child, starved for growing green things, it tasted like a company banquet—far better than any of those bounteous meals she had eaten just before she left her eastern home.

That *was* a feast! Lucretia Ann ate and ate. She ate long after she knew her mother, had she been there, would have been frowning across the table in a manner which would have meant: "Do not be a greedy pig, Daughter." There were two plump ears of corn left. Mrs. Norris pressed them upon her company, but polite Lucretia Ann, now fearful of being thought unmannerly, refused the luscious treat. When later she saw Mrs. Norris scraping it out to the chickens, she felt like crying. She remembered that wasted corn long after she forgot far more important happenings of the journey.

Mrs. Norris and her small friend visited all afternoon with the travelers from the East. When time for the evening meal drew near they started to the little cottage, for there were chickens to feed, and a cow to milk, and baby pigs were grunting about, waiting for their supper.

Little Lucretia Ann felt very much dressed up. Mrs. Norris had washed and ironed the clothing which had taken a plunge into the river. Mother had drawn from the large clothes chest her small daughter's best ruffled calico apron, her snowiest stockings, and her dainty kid strap slippers. The apron was a pretty buff, covered with sprigs of blue and brown flowers, and Lucretia Ann had always admired it greatly. Her hair was curled in many glistening ringlets, and altogether she felt almost like the old-time little girl who had seemed almost lost these past tiresome weeks. She walked primly and daintily, proud of her company attire.

"Pride goeth before destruction, and a haughty spirit before a fall," was one of her mother's favorite quotations. Perhaps Lucretia Ann was too proud, and held her head too high this gala afternoon. For, oh, sorrowful tale! the fun of gathering eggs made her forget her finery, and in climbing a picket fence she slipped, and the toe of her strap slipper caught on a picket. She hung, head down, for a moment, and then—poor little gay-sprigged apron! It caught, and broke Lucretia Ann's fall, so that when she bumped to the ground she was hardly hurt at all. But alas and alack! That sweet best apron was almost ruined. Right down the front was a long, jagged tear.

"Lucretia Ann! Lucretia Ann! This is surely

thy unlucky day," said gentle Mrs. Norris. "But dry thy tears. I will mend thy apron with such tiny stitches that thee will hardly know it has been torn at all; and wait—I have something very nice for thee."

Mrs. Norris disappeared into a little dugout cellar, and returned with her hand behind her back.

"If thou wilt stop crying, I will give thee three guesses to find out what I have in my hand for thee. Three guesses."

Every guess was wrong as wrong could be. So Mrs. Norris slowly brought her hand in front of her, and there was a shining bright red apple. Lucretia Ann squealed aloud in her joy, for she did love apples, and this was the first she had seen in months. Red apples on the desert! How wonderful!

"We brought the trees from Ohio when we came five years ago, and are starting an orchard down in the hollow," Mrs. Norris explained to her guest. "These are the first summer apples we have had. Two trees bore a little this July, and there were twenty red apples and fifteen yellow ones. We will have more when the fall trees bear."

"O Mrs. Norris, how good you are to give me one when you have so few," sighed Lucretia Ann. She lovingly held the apple for a long time, rubbing its glowing cheeks, and smelling its spicy odor, while Mrs. Norris was taking almost unseen stitches in the apron. It did seem a shame to eat such a fragrant beautiful thing. When she did, however, taking the tiniest bites to make it last longer, she felt that she had never tasted such a sweet crisp apple.

Beautiful days must end. Late that night Lucretia Ann cuddled beside her mother in the light spring wagon, and told her all about the wonderful day. She felt that as long as she lived she would hold in her memory the picture of a gay, grey little lady, standing in a garden of bright flowers, waving a cheery farewell until the bend of the river hid the charming picture from sight.

Lucretia Ann wished she were back in Grandmother Pettigrew's arbor eating early peaches and drinking raspberry shrub with cool, tinkling ice in it.

CHAPTER FOUR

EARLY the next morning the wagons were again crawling along the hot sun-parched desert. To the large bird, sluggishly circling above, the caravan might have looked like a giant lizard slowly creeping as it lazily basked in the sun. The memory of that visit with the dear Quaker lady was to Lucretia Ann like a gleaming pearl on a string of drab beads, representing tiresome days.

Lucretia Ann told the story of that happy time again and again to Dimmis, who had been slightly ill that day, and unable to join in the fun. Oh, how Dimmis mourned when Lucretia Ann recounted all those joys!

"Dimmis," said Lucretia Ann, "it was a burning shame that you could not be with me. You saw my dear little Quaker lady, but you did not see the dear little house or all the dear little things in it. But I'll tell you what, Dimmis! When I'm grown I shall have one like it, and you may live with me. We will have the same kinds of flowers, with thousands of morning-glories hanging all about the door. There will be a cat, and a goldie canary which sings all day, and we will invite little girls to come and play with us, just as she invited me. But remember, Dimmis, if we have corn for dinner, or anything else they very much like, and when we pass it they say, 'No, thank you,' just as though they were trying to be polite, don't pay a bit of attention. Just put it on their plates and say:

" 'Why, dearie, surely you can eat another ear. You do not want this wasted.' "

"I'll do that, and I'll truly live with you if your home is shady and cool, Lucretia Ann. My, won't you be glad when this journey is over?"

"I will. When we started out, we thought it was so much fun we would never grow tired, and we laughed because people talked of the terrible trip across the desert. But we are finding out, aren't we?"

Indeed they were finding out. Each day the desert seemed to grow greyer and dustier, and the sun to shine brighter and hotter. The hundreds of heavily loaded wagons which had preceded them had cut the road into such deep ruts that the dust often reached to the hubs of the wheels. The wagons went jigiddy, jig! bumpity bump! and rolled like ships on a stormy sea. It was almost pleasanter to walk than to ride, even if you were tired, your feet cracked and blistered, and your head scorched by the sun. It was bad enough for the wagons and horsemen who were two or three abreast at the head of the train, but it was terrible for those in the rear who must travel all day long in rolling clouds of stifling dust, stirred up by the wagons ahead, and the horses and cattle behind.

One evening, after a trying day, Lucretia Ann was perched wearily on a small mound of earth, long ago thrown up by some desert animal. She listlessly watched preparations for the night, as she had watched them dozens of times before. The wagons were drawn up in a giant circle and linked together forming an enclosure where campfires were made and tents pitched. This was a precaution against surprise attacks by Indians. Mounted guards watched all night the large number of horses and cattle which grazed outside the enclosure. Mercy! Such shouting and dust and noise and confusion!

Lucretia Ann threw her sunbonnet on the ground, pushed back her mop of sweaty curls from her face, and breathed a long, deep sigh. With her chin in the palms of her little brown hands, and elbows on knees she watched her mother prepare the evening meal. Three large poles were crossed to form a tripod, from which, on a chain was suspended an iron kettle in which Mrs. Prence was stirring corn-meal mush. While this cooked she boiled coffee, and fried thick slices of bacon in a long-handled spider, skillfully turning them at just the right moment to keep them

from getting too brown. When they were done, she dropped spoonfuls of the mush into the steaming fat, frying it deliciously crisp. There was plenty of milk, for Mr. Prence, much to Tom's disgust, was taking several cows across the plains, and he had his daily, detested job of milking, which he had hoped to escape upon this trip.

There was also butter, and Lucretia Ann always laughed with glee when churning time came, for she fared much better than Tom with the milking. That had often been her job at home, and some-

66

times she got so tired of this same job that she gave the big stone churn vicious little kicks when no one was looking. At other times she made up games as she stood in the icy springhouse with a big apron tied about her neck to keep the splash of cream away. Up and down, up and down, up and down, she pumped the dasher, millions of times it seemed to her. For Mother was famous for her sweet yellow butter, and always insisted that the cream be *just so cool,* and churned *just so long,* and she never would pour in little streams of hot water to hasten the coming of the butter when it was slow about gathering, as some of the other little girls' mothers did. No, Mother must have firm, yellow granules, which were pressed into sweetest butter which was worked long to press out all the water, and then molded in fancy shapes.

But now all this was changed. No more tiresome churning for little Miss Lucretia Ann. The oxen worked for her. Father fixed a tightly covered bucket which swung under the wagon, and the rolling and jogging soon churned the cream, which had been cooled as much as possible over night. The butter was often poor in quality, owing to the hot weather, but at that it made a most welcome addition to the all too slender fare.

Mother dished up the food she had been cooking, added a large jar of dried-apple sauce, and sounded the call for supper. But Lucretia Ann could not eat. Even the sight of the hot, greasy food seemed to make her ill.

"What is the matter, small Daughter," queried Father anxiously. "You are not touching your supper."

"It is too warm to eat, and I am too tired," sighed the weary little girl, "I wish I were back with my nice Quaker lady, eating some of her sweet red apples. Or else I wish I were back in my Grandmother Pettigrew's yard, having supper in the arbor."

"What would you have, Sister?" inquired Tom.

Lucretia Ann's face became all animation as she visualized the scene.

"Well, let me see—what would we have? First there would be a dish of cool cucumbers, for those are the things Grandmother likes best of all. Then there would be crispy lettuce, and perhaps new potatoes from her garden, and corn. In the very middle of the table she would have her silver butter dish that has the cow with the long horns on top. I am sure there would be a plate of the cold sliced ham which Grandmother bakes with brown sugar and spices stuck in the sides. The green glass dish would have quince jelly in it, all quivery and cold, and there would be spiced currants, for she says they must always be served with ham. There would be a plate of those early peaches which ripen against the stone wall. Grandmother keeps them in a covered pail sitting right in the water in the springhouse, and they are sometimes so cold they make my teeth ache. We would have tall glasses filled with raspberry shrub with large pieces of ice tinkling against the sides——" The child spoke so enthusiastically, and put such feeling into the telling of her story of the good things she would eat that Tom and Stephen both groaned.

"Hey there, Sis," pleaded Tom with both hands clasping his stomach, "are you trying to make a fellow fall dead with hunger? Have a little mercy, won't you? Some things are more than one can stand."

Father smiled and said:

"Just you wait, little lady, until we reach the new home. If all the tales of wondrous fruits and vegetables which grow there are true, you will open your eyes in wonder. We, too, will have raspberry shrub with tinkling ice, and the most delicious fruits. I am going to make you the prettiest flower garden from the seeds which Grandmother Pettigrew gave you. That is one of the first things I shall do next spring, so that you may have your own New England flowers blooming under that bright blue sky. Won't that be fine?"

"It will, Father. I will love my garden. Now if you will please excuse me, I shall get little Faith Greensleave and play with her. She frets so much, and is happy when I play with her."

Dainty Faith crowed and stretched forth her hands with joy at the sight of Lucretia Ann who said:

"Come on, Faithie. Let us take kitty and climb into the back of the wagon. He and I will sing you to sleep."

After a hearty romp, Faith was glad to cuddle down in her small friend's lap, and listen to Lucretia Ann's gentle crooning, and Benjamin's happy purr. She was soon sleeping sweetly, and Lucretia had just placed her comfortably among the bedding when she saw in the distance a heavy cloud of dust which showed that horsemen were approaching. Even the children had been trained to be alert for Indians, so she hastily jumped from the wagon and called:

"Father, I think the Indians are coming! There's a big dust over the plains, and it does not come from the trail, either."

There was hustle and bustle. All could plainly see the horsemen galloping toward them, but clouds of dust and falling twilight prevented them from seeing how many were in the party.

Caravaners must always be on the alert. Quick with the firearms! Quick with the women and children, that they may be protected!

Mr. Prence and Mr. Greensleave went forward to meet the oncomers. The galloping stopped. The dust cleared. There was a relieved laugh as a general handshaking started. Lucretia Ann's "Indians" were two tired plainsmen who were out of provisions and had come down from the hills towards the trail, hoping to meet in with a caravan. They were gay-looking fellows attired in fringed buckskin shirts and breeches, with broad hats, and with jaunty handkerchiefs fluttering about their

necks. The Easterners and Westerners had much news of interest to exchange, and until late in the evening a group sat chatting of the Old World and the New.

Tom, Stephen, and the other boys were greatly delighted when they found that the men had been in Idaho. They plied them with all sorts of questions, and listened to their tales of Indians, of the pioneers, and of the discovery of gold.

"Right there in southwestern Idaho, not so many miles from where you are going, rich placer mines were found. Men came rushing in by the hundreds and thousands; men afoot and men ahorseback. There were men so poor they didn't know where grub for the next meal was coming from, and men with plenty of money. That was a time! Me and Jake was there! I wish you could have seen the gold dust some of those fellows carried away," said the elder of the two.

"How much did you get?" asked Tom breathlessly.

"Nary a bit. Not me and Jake. We had a mule train and packed in supplies. Then we got tired and lit out. But hundreds who found no gold stayed in the Snake River Valley and felt they had something even better. They started farming, dairying, and raising fruits and vegetables. Boys, you'd hardly believe it if I'd tell you of the things

72

that land will grow. Apples 'bout as big as your heads, peaches, pears, prunes——"

"There, didn't I tell you so, Lucretia Ann," Father broke in.

"You didn't tell her wrong. It's true, little gal, and you'd smile to see the way they make things grow. Not with rain from the sky, for there are often two or three months when there is no rain, but with water from the river. They build big ditches and canals, and from these, little ditches which flood water onto the gardens every few days. That, with all the sunshine and good soil, makes things grow like magic. Like to see it, eh?"

"Indeed I would," smiled Lucretia Ann.

Then she leaned against her father's knee and listened drowsily, almost asleep. Suddenly something caught her interest. The strangers were talking of a short cut-off, a trail which would save some miles and which ran most of the way beside a cool, wooded river.

"It's like this, brothers," said the older of the strangers, marking on the ground with a stick to show how the cut-off ran, "this here trail might be the corner of a square, and the cut-off goes cat-a-corner, and most of the way by a river. It's an old Indian path, and I've ridden over it myself in the old days."

"Why do not all the caravans go that way if it is so much better?" queried Mr. Prence.

"Dunno. Habit. Custom. The first comers didn't know about it, and it's always easier to follow the beaten path. The cut-off starts a mile up the trail, and if you fellows want to take it we'll guide you for our grub."

A general discussion followed. Some advocated following the trail; many favored the cut-off, for this was an unusually dry summer and food for the livestock was increasingly difficult to get, as the hundreds of cattle and horses that had gone ahead of them had eaten the grass close. Water, also, was becoming each day more scarce. Dry camps at night were frequent, and it was hard to keep enough water in the barrels which each wagon carried to quench the thirst of men and animals.

Lucretia Ann tugged at her father's sleeve. He leaned down and she patted his cheek gently as she whispered in her most coaxing voice:

"Father, wouldn't it be nice to travel by the shady river? I get so hot and tired on these dreadful days. The water in the barrel tastes so bad. We could walk in the water on the edge of the river where it was shallow, and drink all we wanted of nice cool water every day."

Mr. Prence looked sorrowfully at his daughter.

Could this languid, sun-browned little girl be the laughing, dancing, sparkling Lucretia Ann who seemed to bubble with laughter and joy? How hard the trip was for all, but especially the women and children! No wonder the men grasped at any straw which would ease the weariness of the journey. So he offered little objection when the captain finally decided to take the cut-off, though he lay awake far into the night, wondering if the caravaners had done right in agreeing to take the word of a stranger and seek an unbeaten path?

If the way was so superior, *why did not all the emigrant trains follow it?*

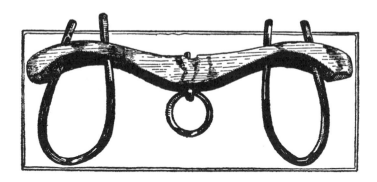

Water! Water! Everybody come as fast as you can hurry! Water!

CHAPTER FIVE

THE camp was astir at the first break of the cool, grey dawn, and by seven the bugle call announced that the caravan was on its way. For several miles the cut-off was a great improvement on the trail; it was, as the stranger said, less dusty because less traveled. But it was only a single file trail, and as the caravan advanced the sagebrush grew denser and denser. By mid-afternoon it was necessary to force the oxen to break their way through the sage. There was no sign of water, and a dry camp was made. Mr. Prence wondered more than ever if the stranger knew whereof he spoke.

Another day passed in the same manner. Outriders scoured the desert for water, but found no spring, creek, or river. The danger of a water famine was acute, and every drop must be conserved. It was becoming plain that if the stranger had ever gone over this trail, it was years ago with Indians on swift ponies. He was as bewildered and at sea as the others. There was not water enough left to risk returning to the point from which they had made the detour.

When another night came the water was practically gone, and several of the party were ill from thirst. Riders returning from all directions still reported no water. The cattle and horses were driven to a little ravine half a mile away where some remnants of dry grass might provide feed.

The night was unbearably hot. Lucretia Ann could not eat she was so weary and thirsty. Oh, for a drink from Grandmother Pettigrew's icy spring. She was too feverish and restless to sleep. But towards morning a slightly cool breeze crept over the camp; it kissed the child's roughened, flushed cheeks, and she drowsed. She dreamed that she was in Grandmother Pettigrew's arbor, and that large raindrops were tumbling down upon her best plaid dress.

"Let me in the house, Grandmother," she thought she was calling. "I do not want to spoil my lovely dress."

She awoke, certain that she heard the drip, drip of falling water, and had smelled the scent of rain. She sat up, peered at the big round moon which was sinking down at the edge of the desert, and sniffed the air again and again.

"I know I smell water; every time a little wind blows by it brings a whiff. I heard it too, and I am going to see," she resolved.

She crept from the wagon and ran breathlessly to the little hill from which she was certain the water had gushed forth. There was a song of happiness in her heart that she could give comfort to so many suffering people.

When she reached the hillside all she saw in the moonlight was black lava rock, thirsty and dry, and straggling greasewood. She looked at the heavens for signs of rain, but dawn revealed a cloudless sky.

"I was sure it was water. I was sure," she said in bewilderment.

Then little Lucretia Ann Prence, in her long-sleeved, high-necked white nightie sat down upon a large black rock, with the first flush of dawn showing up her figure in sharp relief, and cried in her bitter disappointment. Finally she crept back to bed. Again the breezes ruffled her soft curls, and again she fell into a troubled sleep, and again she awoke with the certainty that she had smelled water. She was sure that she heard a faint tinkle like a tiny bell—just the sound a baby waterfall makes when the water splashes from a distance into a tiny pool.

Lucretia Ann sat bolt upright.

"*I did smell water*, and I *heard* it too. No one can make me think I did not, and I'm going to hunt." The small child's lips were set tight, and her head held at its most defiant angle.

The camp was beginning to stir, and Lucretia

Ann slipped quickly into her clothing, and ran to her father.

"Father," she cried, "I dreamed I heard running water, and I smelled it. I got up in the night and looked, but there was nothing but the dry hill. I went to sleep, and I smelled it again when I woke, and I am sure it is behind those large rocks. Get your pail and let us hunt while Mother is getting breakfast. Come, Father, please, just up this hill a little way."

"Daughter, scouts have been all over this territory hunting. We cannot hope to find water when they have failed. Some of them are experienced travelers, and they are hunting now. I see no signs of water, for this creek bed has been dry for months."

"Father, people do find things where other people can't. You must come for just a little while. I know there is water for I did smell it and hear it. I am so thirsty and tired."

Mr. Prence could not resist the pleading little face.

"All right, Daughter, we will look while the camp is rousing. We cannot leave anyway, until the scouts return with their reports."

"Paul, you do humor that child far too much," said Mrs. Prence fretfully. "Do not be away long as we need your help here."

"Get a big bucket, Father. I have my little pail," said Lucretia Ann confidently.

Father hunted his largest bucket to please her, and the two started up the barren slopes. For a few hundred yards they followed the dry creek bed in the rocky little gulch which sloped down from the low foothills beyond. In the springtime this was undoubtedly filled with water which leaped and foamed over these polished rocks, but now even the stones seemed steaming with heat from the morning sun, early as it was.

Up, up, up. Soon they came to a huge lava boulder which obstructed the creek bed. Reluctantly father made the detour around this, and they came again to the sandy creek bed. Again they climbed, and a few yards higher were more rocks. When they had clambered around these, Father noticed what had escaped Lucretia Ann's eye.

The sand was slightly damp in several spots.

"Daughter," he cried excitedly, "do you notice that this sand is a little damp? Perhaps we are nearing water."

"I know we are! Listen, Father, let's listen. Hark! Hush! There! Don't you hear a sound like the drip of water?"

"Perhaps I do," he replied, listening intently.

There certainly was a trickling, dripping sound.

Father and daughter were trembling with excitement. They made haste so rapidly that Lucretia Ann repeatedly stumbled and fell. Finally, rounding another large boulder, they came upon a little waterfall which fell with a thread of silvery water into a pool hollowed from the solid rock. From there it overspread the gravel near by, and the surplus was either licked up by the greedy sand, or soaked through some porous lava rock, and perhaps joined another underground stream farther down the valley. So near the camp, and yet so far.

"It's here, Father, it's here! Now I can drink all I want. O Father!"

Father was down on his knees with his eyes raised to heaven. He realized, as his little daughter fortuntely had been unable to do, just what another day without water would have meant to the caravan.

"Drink but little at first, Lucretia Ann. Oh, how icy cold and clear it is! I will dip with your small pail into my bucket. We will carry down all we can to quench the worst thirst of the folks. Oh, the Lord be praised for guiding you here, my dear little Daughter."

Carefully they dipped the water until the big pail was full, the little pail was full, and even the tin cup was full. By this time the miniature pool

was empty, but the faithful tiny waterfall, as it issued from the rock, was still singing its happy tune of joy that it had come from the gloomy dark into the shining light.

"O Father, isn't this like the happy ending of a fairy tale? Let's walk quietly into camp, just as though nothing had happened, and then surprise the folks by giving them the water. Won't it be fun? I want to let Mother have the first drink, and then little Faith Greensleave. Father, she's sick because she needs plenty of cool water. I will give some to Stephen and Tom, and my nice kitty can have a little, can't he, Father? Even if people are supposed to come first? It wasn't a dream, was it, though everyone thought I was foolish. If I wasn't afraid of spilling this, I could dance all the way down the hillside. Aren't you just bursting with joy, Father?"

"Indeed I am, Daughter. Happy and thankful enough so that I could dance with you; but, as every drop of water counts, we had best express our joy in some other way."

It was a sad, discouraged camp that the two viewed from the rocks above. Mothers were trying to prepare breakfast, but what can one get without water? Children were crying, and an air of dense gloom and fear hung about the whole camp. Lucretia Ann forgot her plans for surprising them all, and as she stood high on a little rock almost directly above, she shouted:

"Water! Water! Water! Everybody come as fast as you can hurry. Water!"

Water! People could not believe their ears, but Father raised his bucket high, and added his call:

"Bring your cups, friends. Water! Water!"

How they all came running at his call, unable to believe the good news! Women and children first.

Such shouting! Such cheering! People who a minute before had seemed too ill and discouraged to move, were running and jumping for joy. When Father told the story little Lucretia Ann was lifted on the shoulders of some of the young men and carried triumphantly about the camp, and hugged and kissed and praised until she longed to run and hide.

Mr. Prence explained how small a stream was flowing, and how every drop must be conserved to satisfy the pressing needs of the party. A bucket brigade was formed, with Father leading the way. Men, women, and children with buckets were placed at intervals up the hill. Father took his place at the spring, and Lucretia Ann, Mother, and Tom took turns in helping dip the water from its rocky cup into small buckets, and pouring it into the large one, which, when filled, was passed down the hill, and other buckets handed back to Father. Each family in turn supplied its needs, and there was a small amount for those animals which were suffering the worst.

That noon, outriders returned with the news that the river had at length been located, much nearer than it was supposed it could be, and the cattle were at once driven out that they might reach the water. The caravan followed the next morning, and toward evening camped by a heavily wooded river, with sandy shores and grassy banks.

"This looks like Heaven, doesn't it, Mother?" sighed Lucretia Ann in bliss, as she paddled her feet, splashed her face, and ducked her head again and again in the cooling waters.

"At least I think we can know how the Israelites felt when they reached the Promised Land," replied Mother.

The camping place chosen was only a short distance from the Oregon Trail, and the emigrants decided to stay there several days until the sick were well, and all should have recovered from the terrible experience. The livestock needed rest, and could feed upon the plentiful grass, drink their fill of water, be re-shod and gather fresh energy for the remainder of the journey. The men would hunt, fish, rest, and tinker with many odd jobs of repair.

While the women! How they rejoiced at every chance to be really clean. For many of them were real New England housewives, with a tradition of cleanliness to uphold, and the lack of water and time for scrubbing had been a sore trial.

Lucretia Ann had more than once heard good Mrs. Greensleave dismally complaining:

"If I'd a known that I'd be grudged the time and denied the water with which to wash even my family and their clothes, I'd of set my foot down right at the start, and never budged a step, so there!"

Little Lucretia Ann rejoiced with the others that they were safe and could rest for a few days in so beautiful a spot. Scrubbed and clean, from the top of her shining curls to the tips of her calloused little toes, she slipped into a fresh white nightie, and lay down to sweet sleep, sniffing hungrily the smell of fragrant grasses, clover, and wild flowers, listening to the happy rippling of the river and the cunning cheep of a drowsy bird.

A few feet away lay Benjamin curled in a fluffy ball, and occasionally twitching his ears and paws as he dreamed of some of the fat mice in the New England barn where he used to play. He thought that dozens of them were scampering about, daring him to catch them. It was a veritable cat's

paradise. Their sleep might not have been so peaceful if they could have foreseen the exciting adventure that this same beautiful river was to bring to them. And all on account of the bad little cat who was curled near his mistress in such an innocent, fluffy ball.

*Wasn't that the jolliest kind of a birthday,
anyway?*

CHAPTER SIX

WHEN Lucretia Ann awoke after hours of beautiful sleep she felt bewildered and her eyes widened with wonder. What could be the matter? The sun was high in the sky, and yet she was as quiet as though in her own trundle bed at home. Why were they not bumping along that rutty old trail? Then she remembered that the caravan was to camp several days in these green pastures, and that there would be long delightful hours of play beside these laughing waters.

"I must get up this minute. I have lost loads of fun already by being such a sleepy head," she said. "I must not waste one more minute of this lovely time."

Then her eyes opened even wider. Last evening she had hung on the wagon bows, just as Mother had taught her, the grey and white calico dress, the limp sunbonnet and the drab stockings, with the heavy, scuffed little shoes underneath. They were gone. In their place a jaunty bright red calico, all tucks and ruffles, swayed by a tiny breeze waved joyfully to Lucretia Ann. It seemed to say:

"Good morning! Good morning! little Miss Lucretia Ann Prence." Underneath the dress lay

93

a stiff red sunbonnet, two pairs of scarlet hose knit
from finest yarn, and a pair of pretty shoes with
red morocco tops. Lucretia Ann sat bolt upright.
Was this an enchanted wagon? Had the fairies
been busy?

Mother was not in sight, but a hum of voices from the river, and the bright array of quilts and clothing of every kind hanging from bushes and trees, and spread upon the grass made her rightly guess that the whole camp was indulging in a general cleaning, airing, and washing.

"Mother must mean that I shall put on these pretty things, for my others are gone, and she must be washing them. But how could she have gotten me a new dress out here in the desert? Is she a magician, and did she wave a wand?"

Lucretia Ann put on the fresh underwear, the darling little flouncy dress, the brilliant stockings, and the shiny shoes. She ran a comb through her newly washed hair which caught gleaming tints from the sun. She was like a drab little wren transformed into a singing red bird. The long inset pockets in the skirt seemed heavy, and the child slipped her hands inside. Then she found that a really, truly fairy godmother had been busy, and that the finery was from dear Grandmother Pettigrew, who loved gay things just as much as did her granddaughter. She had planned this surprise months in advance for a birthday gift. You could hardly imagine a child forgetting her very own birthday, but that is what Lucretia Ann had done in the hardships of that trip.

In each pocket of the dress there was a package

of pink rock candy, with ever so many kinds of hard lozenges. Sweeter than these was the three-cornered note from Grandmother Pettigrew, which said in part:

"A happy, happy birthday to my darling little Lucretia Ann. Grandmother felt sure that you would like some new, cheery clothes to wear on the journey, when the dust is deep, and the days are long. These are to wear every day. Think of your loving grandmother when you put them on, won't you, Child of my Heart?"

"Is there another grandmother in the whole world who would have thought of anything quite so nice?" she exclaimed delightedly. "Oh, I love her, and I love them, but I do not need them to make me think of Grandmother. Mother will think them too bright, and will talk to me about vanity! But I will not be vain—just happy."

The pleased child gave her curls a happy shake, and then skipped from the wagon in search of her family. Light as a wind-blown scarlet leaf she flew over the camp, until she found her mother, and Dimmis, and all the others to whom she could display her new finery. They shouted, "Happy birthday! Lucretia Ann. Happy birthday! Happy birthday!" and admired the new little dress, the scarlet stockings, and the morocco-topped shoes just as much as could be desired. Even Mother, seeing her daughter's sparkling face, did not give the expected warnings against pride, though she did say, "My, child! your garments are so gorgeous they fairly hurt my eyes."

Wasn't that the jolliest kind of a birthday, anyway? All the water you wanted to drink! No jogging along a burning trail! All the fresh meat you possibly could eat, for the men had gone hunting and returned laden with fresh buffalo. There was the fragrance of foods boiling and baking and steaming and frying. Mother managed to gather material for a cake, and in the afternoon Lucretia Ann gave a party. All sorts of odd little gifts, which had been tucked away in stray corners, were brought, and it did seem as though a day could never hold more joy. It ended with a huge bonfire, songs, storytelling, and games.

And now, naughty Benjamin, who seemed born to trouble as the sparks fly upwards, caused the little Lucretia Ann what was probably the great adventure of her whole life.

After two more days by the rippling river, which greatly rested the entire party, the camp was astir before sunup, putting the finishing touches to the packing for the start. Lucretia Ann, in her gay, gay finery, and Dimmis Greensleave, her thin little face alight with happiness, came skipping up.

"Mrs. Prence," Dimmis exclaimed, breathlessly, "Mother has fixed the nicest place in the back of the wagon where Lucretia Ann and I can ride and finish the games we started yesterday. May she journey with us today?"

"I am willing, Dimmis. But we are at the front of the caravan, and will not get the dust. Hadn't you better ride with us? I have also a treat for the noon meal, as I used some of the buffalo fat to make dried-apple and raisin pies. However, you children may do as you please about riding. Ask your mother what she thinks, Dimmis. At any rate, wherever you decide to ride, you had better eat lunch with us."

"Thank you, Mrs. Prence, I shall talk to Mother," returned Dimmis politely.

"All right, Mother, we will be back for lunch, if we ride in the Greensleave wagon. Dimmis, you run and ask your mother about it, and then meet me at the river. I want to feed Benjamin some more meat, and make him take a drink. Come on, Benjamin, do you want more liver, or did you stuff too much yesterday?"

The girls met at the riverbank for a farewell wade, while the cat was eating his meal. They decided that they would ride in Dimmis' wagon that morning, then eat lunch with the Prences, and ride with them during the hotter afternoon.

Benjamin was feeling frolicsome that morning. After eating, and drinking of the sparkling water, he started trying to catch the grasshoppers which were whirring along the bank of the stream, and playing hide-and-seek among the dry grasses. The girls laughed at his antics awhile, and then Lucretia Ann said:

"Come, Dimmis, let us put on our shoes, and get Benjamin and put him in his cage. He has on one of his bad streaks this morning, and Father will be very cross if he delays the caravan again, as he did the other morning. He thinks we shouldn't have brought Benjamin, I am sure, and he did it to please me. Here kitty, kitty, kitty. Come, Benjamin."

The cat loved to tease his worried mistress, and he had had far too many dull, thirsty days in that old cage at the back of the wagon, to want any more of them. This delightful spot, so full of good things to eat, exactly suited him. He gave the girls a wicked wink, switched his tail, and like a flash was bounding up the river and over a long hill. The more the girls chased him, the faster Benjamin ran. Several times he stopped just beyond their reach, and looked at them knowingly, just as if he were saying, "Aren't we having a lovely frolic, friends?" Lucretia Ann, at the end of her patience cried:

"Benjamin, I have a mind to go and leave you. Come on, Dimmis, let's leave him, and maybe a great, awful, *howly* coyote, or a terrible *Indian* with a huge tomahawk will get him! O kitty, kitty, kitty, do come!"

Again a long, long chase, in which swift little Dimmis finally gained and fell headlong, grasping onto Benjamin's tail. Hard and fast she held until Lucretia Ann came and imprisoned him in her full skirts.

"Lucretia Ann," gasped Dimmis, red faced and angry, "I can't see why you have such a terrible cat. I pulled his tail hard, when I had him."

"I am glad you did, only he might have scratched you," was the breathless reply.

The children sat panting on the grassy bank, great drops of sweat falling from their brows.

"Benjamin," lectured Lucretia Ann, emphasizing her words with a heavy shake, "you are the worst cat. If you knew how near Father came to leaving you in Vermont, you would try and be nice."

Benjamin did not mind either the shake or the scolding. He had had his fun, and was content to fold his paws daintily under his chin, snuggle down in his mistress' lap, and gently lick her sunbrowned hands, as he loudly purred.

"Isn't that the cunningest thing! I can't be

cross at him. He looks just like a baby," smiled Lucretia Ann. "Let's rest a minute before we go back."

"All right," agreed Dimmis. "If we had a place to put the cat, we could wade just a tiny minute. I think I have never been warmer, and I know I have never seen such sparkly white sand."

The child clutched a handful, lifted it high above her head, and let it sift slowly through her fingers, watching it brighten with the sunlight, until it seemed a shower of pearls. Lucretia Ann lazily watched it fall, and then suddenly laughed aloud.

"I'll tell you what, Dimmis! Benjamin needs to be punished, he's been so bad. Let's make a jail, and put him in. There are lots of those large flat rocks. Then we can paddle our feet in the water, and he cannot run away."

"Won't that be fun?" gleefully agreed Dimmis.

By careful arrangement they managed to interlock the rocks so that they did not topple over. Then Lucretia Ann held Benjamin in the prison with one hand, while with the other she helped Dimmis place a very large slab across the top of the cave. Benjamin crouched meekly in his cell, and peered curiously through the open cracks.

The chums spent some time cooling their feet in the ripples of the river, but at last decided they must run back over the hill to the caravan. Just then, however, they spied, a little farther up the river, a tree laden with something red and alluring.

"As sure as I am alive, those are wild plums," exclaimed Lucretia Ann. "Shall we stop and get them?"

"Let's be sure what they are first. If they are plums we can take them back to camp. Should we stop, though?" inquired Dimmis.

"I think we can hurry. It will take but a moment, and then we will run all the way. The folks will be so pleased to have a taste of fruit."

There were but a few handfuls of the plums, yet it took the girls some time to gather them. Then, all of a sudden, Lucretia Ann was panic stricken.

"Dimmis," she cried, "do you see how high the sun is? And the folks planned to leave so early this morning. I know it is time to go. Perhaps everyone is waiting for us."

"We have not heard the bugle. It blows when we should be starting," said Dimmis.

"No, that's true. But it will blow any minute. You carry the plums in your apron, and I will carry Benjamin, and we will run as fast as our legs will carry us. I don't know, Dimmis, about riding in your wagon. It is getting so terribly hot that maybe we had better ride in front."

"Maybe," panted Dimmis. Her little legs were spinning over the ground, she was spilling plums as she ran, and her heavy black braids were flapping with every step. Lucretia Ann was behind, for Benjamin wanted to run on his own feet, and was struggling to get down. But she was hurrying to keep up, and her scarlet ruffles fluttered like poppy petals in the breeze, and her myriads of sunny ringlets stood on end. Both felt terribly frightened, terribly lonely, though why, they could not say.

There was reason enough for their alarm. Silence—deep, deep silence—greeted them. Not a prairie schooner, not a person, not even a straggling dog in sight! Where early that morning had been bustling activity, there was absolute quiet. Indeed, the girls might have thought they had mistaken the spot, save for the trampled grass and remains of burnt-out campfires. There was even no sign of dust in the distance, so the train was evidently on its way, and with it were the two smaller trains which had overtaken the party the previous night.

Neither child could believe her eyes. What terrible mistake was this? Lucretia Ann first found her voice.

"Dimmis, they've gone! Our fathers and mothers have left us. I never heard of anything so dreadful."

"And we were away such a tiny, tiny little while. How could they leave their little daughters?"

Neither child could realize that what had seemed to her like short minutes was in reality several hours. Dimmis began to sob wildly.

"They didn't mean to leave us," comforted Lucretia Ann. "Don't cry, Dimmis. I'll tell you what's the trouble. My folks think I am riding with you, and your folks think you are riding with me. You know we did not tell them what we had decided to do. They'll come back for us. But maybe not before night. What is the best thing for us to do?"

"Let's start right now and follow them on foot. Then they will not have so far to come back. If we run like the wind, perhaps we can catch up."

"Would it be safe for us to go walking on the desert without any water? Father said this morning that he thought it would be the hottest day we have had. And I've run so fast now that it seems as if I can never run again. I haven't caught my breath yet. Your face is redder than a beet, and I know mine is too."

"We could drink a lot before we start so we

104

will not get so thirsty, and put wet leaves in our bonnets," said Dimmis. "No, I forgot. We left our bonnets in the wagon."

"If we only had a water jug! Maybe we can make bonnets of leaves and twigs," suggested Lucretia Ann, quite brightened at the thought of something to do. "Come, Dimmis, do not cry. Let us sit down by this tree and plan what we had better do."

Then her eyes fell on Benjamin, the cause of all their grief.

"Benjamin, you wicked cat! You got us into all this trouble. Help us get out of it now. Think of something to do," she demanded.

A clatter of rocks now startled the girls. They

looked down the river in the opposite direction from which they had come.

Riding straight towards them were a number of Indians, gay in their colored blankets.

Indians! Indians! Run! Hide! Run!

CHAPTER SEVEN

"RUN! Run! Hide!" screamed Dimmis. "Hush, don't be silly!" admonished Lucretia Ann, grabbing Dimmis and giving her a shake to bring her to her senses. "These Indians have already seen us, and no matter how fast we run, they can run faster. Let's jump on this big rock and see if our folks are coming back. Maybe they've missed us."

Up, up, the sides of the low, steep rock they clambered, puffing for breath. The delicious plums which had been so carefully gathered were forgotten and slipped from Dimmis' apron to the ground in a crimson heap, where they were later seen and eaten with glee by the Indians. Benjamin howled as Lucretia Ann held him tightly under one arm. He did not like this hurry and bustle and wanted to get down. With the other arm Lucretia Ann tenderly encircled Dimmis' waist, and stood there bound to protect her from all harm. No signs of dust or a returning caravan or stray horsemen were seen, and even now the whole procession of Indians was upon them. Dozens and dozens of small shaggy ponies plodded up, some carrying riders, and others packed with skins, blankets, bags, and baskets of luggage.

109

From the sides of many of the ponies dragged the long wickiup or wigwam poles, which the Indians carried with them. Between many of them, where they dragged on the ground, were placed skin or woven baskets packed with supplies, or at times holding some of the smaller children, who were resting comfortably and unconcernedly in these unusual vehicles. A rabble of forlorn-looking dogs was in the parade, and they came sniffing around the rock and barking until the Indians drove them back.

"Be polite and smile, Dimmis," said Lucretia Ann with shaking voice. "I heard someone say never to let the Indians know you are scared, and Grandmother Pettigrew says a smile will always make friends. Smile, Dimmis, smile."

"I'll try, Lucretia Ann, but won't they scalp us?"

Such frozen little smiles on white scared faces!

"Of course they won't," said Lucretia Ann crossly, all the more so because she had thought of the same thing, and her heart was pounding with fear. "All the caravaners say that the Indians hereabout are friendly."

Dimmis dried her eyes, and the children stood like two valiant, though trembling statues. It was hard to be brave, for the rock was only a few feet high, and the Indians were coming steadily on.

Their leader rode his horse straight toward them, until it seemed as though he meant to ride over the rock. The girls thought they should have to jump and run, when he reined up sharply and extended a hand, saying "How!"

Each child politely put forth her hand, and now they were surrounded by a crowd of Indians. All stood in stolid, impressive silence for several moments, looking at the children. Then a jabbering and chattering started. The Indians wanted to examine everything, and seemed intensely interested. The scarlet birthday dress especially pleased them, as did the bright stockings, and the gay-topped shoes. One little girl about their own age reached up and carefully ran her hands along the shiny leather. The curls of sunny hair, which the sun lighted until it made a halo about Lucretia Ann's head, seemed particularly amazing to them. And then Benjamin, whom his small mistress had tried to hide, stuck his head out from under her arm to see what was going on, and he was another source of astonishment. At what was evidently a command from one of them Lucretia Ann held him up for them all to see. There was more excited talking, and one boy came too near, grabbed a paw roughly and stepped back quickly with a long scratch across the dirty brown arm. The other Indians laughed, but kept their distance, wondering just what this strange yellow animal might be.

Dimmis' long, glistening braids, which her mother had combed and plaited so carefully that morning, also excited their admiration. Two of the Indians grasped them and stretched them out to their full length to show the others how long they were. Poor little Dimmis felt that her last hour had come.

"They're going to scalp me! They're going to scalp me!" she screamed and sank to the rock in a forlorn, sobbing heap. At this a wrinkled old squaw who had been standing at the outskirts of the circle, pushed her way through the group. She seemed accustomed to commanding, for as she spoke a few words and waved her arms, the Indians stepped back. Several of the more curious of the children did not obey her, and she threateningly raised a stick she carried, which caused them to step quickly aside. She was followed by a younger squaw who had a beady-eyed papoose strapped to a papoose board on her back; she was evidently the mother of the child who had admired the red-topped shoes. The older woman gave little grunts and pats, seemingly to try to reassure the girls that they would not be harmed. Indeed, she seemed to feel just as sorry for them

112

as Grandmother Pettigrew would have felt for a sobbing, frightened Indian child.

Meanwhile, some of the Indians were searching among the trees, and riding short distances up and down the banks of the river, trying to find the white folks to whom these children belonged, and wondering what they could be doing alone here in this deserted spot, for not a tent, wagon, or sign of human being could they find.

These Indians had been with the whites very

little, and knew only a few words of the English language, so there was little chance of the girls making them understand their troubles by speech. The grandmother and Lucretia Ann tried talking by signs. The old squaw first pointed to the Indian girl and her mother, and then to the children, as though asking where their parents were. Lucretia Ann understood, and she in turn did her best by pointing and talking very loudly and distinctly, as though loud speech might help.

"See," she said, pointing to the camping ground, "that's where we camped, and right over there is where our wagon stood. Then my kitty ran away up the river, and of course we didn't want to go without him so we ran too." Here she pointed to the cat and away up the river, at the same time making running motions. "And we played and we played and we forgot how long we had been away. Anyhow we did not hear the bugle blow. When we came back, there was nobody here. Not a soul," she said tragically. "They've gone— gone, down the trail." She pointed and pointed and the grandmother at last seemed to understand the story. By the time it was told, all of them were laughing at their funny attempts to understand one another. The squaws withdrew to a group of men, and talked at length. What was to happen to them the girls could not think. Already part of the Indians had gathered up the river in the direction they were going when they found the children.

"Maybe they'll go off and leave us here just as we were," said Dimmis. "Oh, if they only will I am sure somebody will come for us very soon."

"Well, Dimmis," said Lucretia Ann solemnly shaking her curls, "these Indians are all right, I think, and mean to be kind. I liked that nice old lady. She makes me think of my Grandmother Pettigrew. Perhaps she's a grandmother too."

"Lucretia Ann Prence! What a horrid thing to say! Your grandmother is sweet and clean; she wears such pretty clothes that she looks like a picture. Her hair is so white and curly, and her cheeks pink, and she smells of the good things in her garden. That old lady is a *squaw*. She isn't clean, and she isn't tidy. Her hair is greasy, and there are grease and dirt all over her blanket. She's smelly too. When she came close I could hardly stand it."

"Maybe she is. But I saw her kind eyes and she looked so sorry when you cried. Her hands were so gentle when she patted me. I think she will help us if she can."

Hopefully the children watched the shaggy ponies file one by one up the river, and vanish over the hill where Benjamin had gone. Soon only

115

about a dozen were left: six men, the grandmother, the mother with the little girl and baby, and a boy somewhat older than the chums. The men mounted their ponies. Lucretia Ann was ordered to get on a white pony behind the squaw, and when she protested, the grandmother motioned her almost crossly to do so. She sat there facing the beady-eyed papoose who was strapped to his mother's back. Dimmis was placed behind the little girl whom she and Lucretia Ann later named Dark Fawn from a book they had read, for they never could understand the name by which her mother called her. The Indian child was much interested in the white strangers, and kept abreast of her mother; in fact, most of the time she let her pony wander at his own sweet will so that she might miss nothing of what was going on.

The men started ahead, and the children held their breath in terror as they watched which way they started out. Good luck! The thing that brought great joy to their hearts was the fact that they rode straight ahead on the Oregon Trail, following where their parents had gone.

"Dimmis, do you see?" cried Lucretia Ann excitedly. "These Indians are taking us to our folks; I know they are! Didn't I say they were nice and kind?"

"It's almost too good to be true," replied Dimmis happily.

They would see their parents at any time. Why, almost any moment they might meet them returning. What a wonderful tale they would have to tell. Wouldn't Tom envy them riding with the Indians and everything? Now when he started to brag, his little sister could silence him with a word.

Right cheerfully they rode along. The girls would look at the tracks and hoof prints in the road, and Lucretia Ann would say:

"I'm sure Shorty and Whitey walked here."

And Dimmis would reply:

"I'm sure Bess and Peter made those tracks, for it looks like the feet of our big old oxen." And they giggled and laughed and were so light hearted in their relief that they did not mind the terrible heat or the jolt of the ponies or the fact that they were alone with Indians. Wouldn't it be funny if their folks had not even missed them when the Indians rode up to the caravan? The girls were giggling over this idea when Lucretia Ann noticed something that made her give a quick cry.

"Dimmis, do you see what's happened? We've left the trail, and these Indians are taking us away."

The child tugged violently at the squaw's arm,

and pointed back towards the trail, at the same time starting to jump from the pony. But the Indian held her back, nodding as though trying to reassure her.

Dimmis looked back toward the road—sure enough they were now going at right angles on a narrow trail through the sagebrush. She gave a loud cry and began to sob, saying:

"O Lucretia Ann, they are taking us away, and I am afraid we will never see our mothers again."

The grandmother who was on a pony just ahead heard the sound and turned about to see what was the matter. She stopped her pony, and by many signs and pointings seemed to try to say that all was well.

"Don't cry, Dimmis," said Lucretia Ann soberly. "I think the grandmother is trying to tell us that everything is all right, and I do hope it is. But I wonder where we're going."

For a while the girls rode on in silence, too overwhelmed with this anxiety even to talk. And in fact, it was too hot for speech. Lucretia Ann held tight to Benjamin, who most unwillingly stayed in her arms. Every breath seemed an effort. There was a quiet sultriness in the air and if one glanced over the desert, waves of heat seemed almost visible to the eye. Lucretia Ann could remember how, early that morning, her father had wiped the drops of sweat from his face, which looked worn and tired, and had said:

"I do dread leaving this shady spot, for, unless I am mistaken, this sultriness indicates that we shall have our hottest day. The trail will be almost unbearable."

"Whew! Yes, it is going to be a scorcher all right," neighbor Sparrow had replied, and looking kindly at Lucretia Ann, had said: "Better keep in the shade of the wagon today, little gal, if you don't want to melt down into a grease spot."

Lucretia Ann did not like being called a "little gal," but she did wish she could be near kindly Mr. Sparrow right now. And the day *was* a scorcher. Neither child had any protection from the sun, as their bonnets were in the wagons. Lucretia Ann's face began to look like one of the bright poppies in Grandmother Pettigrew's garden drenched with dewdrops, while Dimmis looked like a fragile wilted violet. The little papoose, who was in front of Lucretia Ann, also looked so warm that the child felt sorry for him.

"Baby," she queried, trying to wipe the drops of sweat from his brown dusty face with her handkerchief, "baby, dear, did you ever know such a hot day before? I do not think you did, as you are not very old, but perhaps you did because you live here. You do not know my Grandmother Pettigrew, and you do not know stoves, and you do not know caraway cookies, I am sure, but if you did, this air feels just like the heat from the oven when Grandmother is baking cookies on a hot summer day. My, I wish I had one! Aren't you about baked?" she called to Dimmis, who was now ahead as the ponies must go single file on this narrow trail.

"I am. Pretty soon the Indians will have baked Dimmis Greensleave to eat. My hair is almost ready to catch on fire. I think I heard it crackle a minute ago. I wish I had my sunbonnet."

"Why don't you wish for something better? I wish I had a mother," shouted Lucretia Ann, for conversation was not so easy now that they were going single file. "I also wish Benjamin would be quiet, and not be so heavy. He is almost breaking my arm."

"Let me carry him. It will be a comfort to have someone I love near me," said Dimmis.

"All right, I will, if you can get that girl to wait a minute. But oh, be careful of my baby, won't you, Dimmis?"

The exchange was finally made, much to Dark Fawn's delight, and then there was another long silence.

A tiny breeze sprang up. It only intensified the heat. Then the wind began to huff and puff, and huff and puff like the old wolf in the story and each huff and puff brought such dark clouds of alkali dust that it was almost impossible to breathe. The children's eyes were blinded by the dust, and they felt as though they should choke. Lucretia Ann was sure that the wind would blow her from her horse, and she clutched tightly to the tattered blanket which was about the squaw.

Now the Indians realized that the storm was too severe for them to continue. They halted, dismounted, tethered their ponies to the sage, and each made himself as comfortable as possible. The grandmother tossed the chums a blanket, and they lay on the ground with it over their heads. They drew their breath as best they could from beneath its stifling folds, and found that this was better than getting the full force of the alkali dust which burned their faces and made their throats sting.

Lucretia Ann felt that in all her nine years she had never been in such a terrible plight. As ever when in trouble, her thoughts flew to Grandmother Pettigrew. She was probably sewing and singing on her shady porch, and the child could almost smell the honeysuckle which was flinging its sweetness over the yard. She could see Grandmother's rosy cheeks and watch the soft flutter of the folds of the fluted fichu. She could almost hear the happy voice as Grandmother sang a gay, gay tune, keeping time with a smart tap, tap of her tiny slippers. Even solemn tunes had a happy lilt when Grandmother sang them.

"Dimmis," said Lucretia Ann suddenly, "what would my darling little Grandmother Pettigrew think if she could see me lying on this awful prairie with the Indians? I think she would be almost frightened to death, for she loves me. Why, why did we leave her? Will I ever see her again?"

"Will I ever see my little sister Faith again? Will we ever see anyone again?" wailed Dimmis.

"I wouldn't have come on this old trip if I had thought the Indians would carry us away," replied Lucretia Ann.

Meanwhile the wind swooped down with renewed force. It whistled and howled through the sage as though it were trying to uproot each separate brush. It mourned, it wailed, and it cried.

"I feel lonely enough without that wind making that terrible sound," shivered Dimmis. "Can't it stop for even a minute?"

And the girls snuggled even closer together, seeking consolation in one another's arms. They took turns holding frightened little Benjamin, who did not like those close quarters at all. His soft pink nose, and his gentle yellow paws snuggled against their necks, and gave them a warm, comfy feeling. As they lay there they wondered how this dreadful, dreadful day would end, and what would be the next thing to happen. They would have held bad little Benjamin even tighter if they could have foreseen how soon he was to be punished for his part in this day's disaster.

There's nothing to do but go where these Indians take us.

CHAPTER EIGHT

FOR an hour or so the storm continued with increasing fury; then it began to die down, and, almost as suddenly as it had come, it faded away. The girls sat up, threw off the blanket, and looked about them at a strange grey world. Through the hazy air the sun seemed like a large coppery red ball suspended in the sky.

The Indians began remounting, giving grunts of disapproval and disgust. Soon the caravan was again picking its way through the sage.

"We are all so covered with this whitish dust, and the air is so full of dust, that we look like a parade of ghosts, don't we?" asked Lucretia Ann.

"We do. It's hard to tell who anyone is when we do see him," agreed Dimmis. "You and Dark Fawn and Big Mouth look just alike. I couldn't tell you one from the other," she giggled.

"You're just as bad," retorted Lucretia Ann. "Nobody would know that your hair is black. Are we going to ride on forever?"

On and on and on! The dust-laden air, the burning heat, the thirst, the hunger, the fright! When the girls felt that they could not live another moment a willow-bordered creek came into view. The company dismounted and refreshed themselves. Lucretia Ann and Dimmis knelt at the edge and drank long and deeply. They ducked their heads, bathed their sun-blistered faces, and rolled up their sleeves and splashed the water up their arms. The Indians noticed the soft little arms, and crowded round, touching the smooth skin and marveling at its wonderful whiteness.

Benjamin enjoyed the cooling stream as much as any of the party. He too crouched by the bank, and his eager little pink tongue lapped daintily at the water.

"I'm afraid Benjamin will have a sunstroke," said Lucretia Ann anxiously. "See how he squints his little eyes. I think I had better put cold water on his head."

In spite of the heat, Benjamin did not take kindly to his mistress' thoughtful care, and Dimmis had to hold him tightly while Lucretia Ann doused his head. He struggled so hard to get away that she was well scratched and let him go, saying angrily:

"He isn't a bit thankful for anything we try to do for him, Lucretia Ann. He *ought* to have a sunstroke."

"I know he's bad," sighed Lucretia Ann, "but I love him, anyway. But aren't you hungry, Dimmis? I am. It must be hours past our lunch time."

"I'm hungry too. Hungry as a bear. But these Indians do not look as though they would have anything I would like to eat. I wonder what the grandmother is doing?"

The grandmother was untying one of two very large woven baskets which were slung from the sides of a shaggy spotted pony. She removed a piece of leather which was tightly tied over the top, and the girls saw the Indians dip their hands into the basket and bring forth fists full of berries —some gleaming red, and others purplish black. They were about the size of the early green goose- berries which Lucretia Ann had often had to pick and stem for pies.

"My! Don't those look good?" she asked of Dimmis. "Whatever can they be? I have never seen anything like them. Do you suppose they will give us some, and will they be fit to eat?"

"The Indians seem to think they are," replied Dimmis. "At least they can't be poison. But would they be clean enough to eat? The Indians picked them, you know."

"There's plenty of water to wash them in," said practical Lucretia Ann.

The grandmother was now beckoning to the children to come nearer, and when they did so she motioned that they should help themselves from the basket. Each took a handful, washed them in

the running water, and then Lucretia Ann doubt-
fully tasted.

"They're good!" she cried joyfully. "Just as
good as berries can be. Eat some, Dimmis."

Fastidious Dimmis was more cautious, but after nibbling several of the berries she agreed with
her friend, and each child ate a number of handfuls of the satisfying fruit. The girls later learned
that this band of Indians was returning from an
expedition into the mountains after huckleberries.
They went there yearly, and sometimes camped
for weeks, eating all the berries they could hold,
drying quantities for winter use, and bringing out
baskets of fresh fruit which they traded for other
articles of food or for clothing.

While eating, the children forgot about their
little cat, who, too, was hungry, and was frisking
about the bank of the stream putting his paws into
the water and trying to catch one of the tiny
minnows which were darting about in a small
pool. But the Indian boy had not forgotten. He
was fascinated with the handsome animal, and he
made his way cautiously into a group of willows
where he could watch Benjamin at play. From
time to time he threw him a scrap of dried fish,
which the hungry cat eagerly pounced on. Once
or twice Lucretia Ann saw him greedily grab up
something, but she supposed he was finding grass-

hoppers, and paid little heed as long as he was near by.

Benjamin was eager for more fish. The boy, whom the girls had christened Big Mouth, on account of the width of his mouth, threw each piece a little closer to the willows. He threw one last offering, and while Benjamin was hungrily devouring it, he sprang from the bushes, grabbed the cat, and ran with swiftest speed toward his pony. Lucretia Ann looked up at the sound of Benjamin's long yowl, and gave chase with Dimmis close behind.

"That's my cat! He's taking my kitty! Give him to me, bad boy!"

"Give us our cat. It's ours. Listen to the poor

131

kitty yowl, Lucretia Ann. Maybe we can catch him."

Big Mouth reached his pony, but as he sprang on her back, he slipped off, handicapped by Benjamin, who was struggling, howling, and trying to scratch.

"Run! He's falling! Hurry! Hurry!" screamed Lucretia Ann. "We'll catch him yet."

But Big Mouth was swift in his movements, and like a flash was again on the wiry little pony, shouting for her to start, just as the girls came up. Lucretia Ann managed to grab one moccasined foot and hung on valiantly. Dimmis, who was just behind, became so excited that she did not know what she was doing, and lay hold of the only thing in sight—the pony's long, slippery tail. Of course it slipped at once from her grasp, and she sat down hard on the prairie. Lucretia Ann held on bravely for a few steps, but the pony was getting up speed, and Big Mouth was giving vicious kicks, so she too had to loose her hold. Miraculously, neither child was hurt. Lucretia Ann stood watching through her tears, and called sadly:

"Good-by, my darling little cat. Maybe I'll never see you again."

"I think you will, honey," soothed Dimmis. "I think that boy just wants to see your cat."

"Oh, I don't know Dimmis. Did you hear the

poor little thing cry, and did you see him try and get away? He doesn't like Indians, and I do not either. Dimmis, everything terrible is happening today."

"I know it, Lucretia Ann. But we have each other, and I love you."

"Yes, but Dimmis, maybe they'll eat my kitty. They eat dogs, and cats are much nicer than dogs. Oh, my poor little cat, you are too cunning to be made into a stew."

Mournfully the children returned to the creek bank, where the fat, comfortable squaw was now holding her baby, whom she had taken from the cradle. She regarded the whole affair a huge joke, and was laughing heartily at the thought of Dimmis trying to stop the pony by grasping her tail.

But the grandmother did not laugh. She looked at the sorrowful little faces, and she patted Lucretia Ann gently on the shoulder and spoke to her. If the guttural words could have been understood they would have meant:

"White child, with hair like the moon, do not cry. I will try and help you get back the animal."

Somehow both children felt comforted.

In a few minutes the party again resumed the journey, and soon Lucretia Ann gave a gasp of relief:

"Dimmis, this looks like the Oregon Trail. I believe we're on the trail again."

"It does look so, but if it's the trail it certainly looks funny. No wagons have gone by here lately, nor any oxen or horses."

"That's true, Dimmis," said her friend soberly. "Our folks haven't passed here today from the looks of things."

The Indians too seemed puzzled. They were gazing up and down the trail, seemingly uncertain which way to go. It was an odd-looking trail, for parts were hard and shiny, as though newly swept clean by a monstrous broom, and others were filled with ridges and hillocks which made the girls think of snowdrifts, only they were of sandy dust. It took some minutes of animated discussion for the Indians to come to their decision. As before, the grandmother seemed to have the deciding voice, and soon the whole line of ponies was trotting in the direction she had chosen.

Lucretia Ann scanned the trail carefully for perhaps half a mile. Then she said decidedly:

"Dimmis, I'm so mixed up that I do not know whether we are going toward the river or away from it. But I do know now why the trail looks so funny. That terrible wind swept the wagon wheel prints and all the other tracks away; so if our folks did pass here before the storm came we would not know it. If they did not, I am sure they missed us when the wind blew so hard, for they would have to stop. Perhaps they have gone back to the river to hunt us. Anyway, let's hope we will see them soon."

"Perhaps we will. There's nothing for us to do but to go where these Indians take us."

"Nothing," agreed Lucretia Ann, "and we'll hope they are taking us to our folks."

Mile after mile passed as the procession moved briskly along, not meeting, or being overtaken by one human being. This was odd, for on many days the trail was the scene of much travel. In late afternoon faint tracks began to appear, and they grew clearer and clearer until it looked just as the girls remembered it before the storm. It was evident that the wind storm had passed this spot, and it was also plain to the children, from the direction of the footprints, that they were still following the trail, and not returning to the river.

"It's getting time for our folks to camp for the night. Maybe we'll see them any time now."

"Maybe. Or, if we do not find our folks, perhaps some other caravan will be camping, and we will stay with them."

But no magic, newly made city of wagons and tents had sprung up by the roadside, and no curls of smoke from cheery campfires gave signs that the cooking of dinner was in progress.

When the sun began to sink behind the edge of the prairie the Indians left the trail and turned toward a river which was running near the road. The horses forded the river, and the party prepared to camp in a dense thicket of trees, well hidden from the trail.

When Lucretia Ann saw what they planned to do, she called to Dimmis:

"Watch Big Mouth every minute. I know he still has Benjamin, for I saw his little head peeking at me a little while ago when that mean boy turned to cross the river. I want him so much."

The Indian lad, however, was too smart for the girls. He was at the head of the line of ponies, while they were at the rear. There was some delay in their crossing, and when they dismounted both boy and cat had vanished. The children fell like wilted little leaves on the cool grass near the riverbank, stretched their tired arms and legs, and found relief from the sultry heat in the cooling shade.

In spite of their loneliness and fear, they watched with interest the preparations for the night. The papoose was hung in his cradle from the limb of a tree, and watched the scene with blinking, unsmiling eyes. Gaudily painted tents, or wickiups, were quickly thrown over the poles which had dragged from the ponies' sides; fires were started, and preparations for the evening meal begun. Soon Big Mouth strolled into camp, a wide grin spreading over his face. The girls ran to him, and begged with signs that he give them the cat. He only stretched his wide mouth the wider, and laughed heartily at their pleading.

"My poor, poor little cat," mourned Lucretia Ann. "Where do you suppose he has put him?"

The children were too tired to care to eat, though the Indians gave them some unappetizing smelling stew, some flat pressed cakes made of the camas, and more of the huckleberries. They huddled together in the hollow of a mighty cottonwood tree which had been struck by lightning, so that one side was burned in and hollowed, making an opening several feet in depth. During the evening the Indians sat round the camp, laughed, joked, and told stories. Dark Fawn and Big Mouth both seemed in high spirits after a hearty meal, and danced round and round the fire, in and out, back and forth, chanting a weird, monotonous war song. They finally persuaded the girls to join in their play. At first they felt most awkward and uncomfortable, but soon all four were winding around, in and out, back and forth, the white children doing their best to imitate the little red brother and sister in the weird chant and the uncertain steps. They forgot for a little while that they were lost, and entered into the fun with zest. Lucretia Ann began improvising new steps, and she made a charming picture as she skipped about, flames from the dying fire occasionally lighting her as she curtsied and dipped, with her scarlet skirts flying. The Indians' applause pleased the child.

"Let's sing for them, Dimmis," she suggested. "Maybe they'll like that, and perhaps the nicer we are to them, the nicer they will be to us."

Joining hands, the friends sang in their soft sweet voices the old favorites they had chorused about the campfires many evenings while on the trail, and the Indians expressed their approval with nods and grunts, demanding more and more. So they sang until their voices were so husky they could sing no more.

"They're being nice to us. They act as if they liked us, don't they?" said Lucretia Ann.

"Indeed they do. I think they do not mean to hurt us."

Now it was growing late, and the Indians were preparing for sleep. The grandmother pointed to a pile of skins and blankets in a corner of the wickiup.

"O Lucretia Ann! We cannot sleep in that

hot, smelly place with so many Indians. Do you suppose the grandmother would let us sleep outside?"

"We can try," said Lucretia Ann. The noble old cottonwood was close to the wickiup, and the girls tugged at a buffalo skin and a light blanket, and spread them under the trees so that their heads would be in the sheltered hollow, and indicated that they would like to sleep there. The grandmother seemed willing, and soon the camp was quiet. The girls could not sleep; a hundred thoughts were running through their heads.

"Our prayers, Lucretia Ann," said Dimmis suddenly. "Now is the time we need to pray, if we ever did."

"Yes," said Lucretia Ann sorrowfully, "and do you remember how bad we were last night when we ran races to see who could get through her prayers first! Perhaps if we'd prayed better we might have remembered to mind our parents, and not rush away as we were told dozens of times not to do."

The two knelt in the hollow shelter of the comforting tree.

"O dear, dear Jesus, help us to find our folks," was the burden of Dimmis' little plea, which she repeated over and over.

Lucretia Ann's prayers varied each night with

her mood. Now she thought of a refrain she had heard Deacon Tracy use dozens and dozens of times and she prayed: "O God of Abraham and Isaac and Jacob, deliver us from bondage." She liked the sound of that last refrain. Over and over she prayed, "Deliver us from bondage," earnestly and fervently. Then the friends lay down, but not to sleep. The stillness when it was still, the noise when it was noisy, terrified them. At times the dogs came sniffing about, barking and snarling. A coyote howled in the distance; overhead a sleepy bird gave an occasional cheep. Once a porcupine whose home they had disturbed went running across their feet!

Then a wailing little wind seemed to be sobbing in the distance; it rustled the bushes as it

came toward them creep, creep, creep, until it seemed about to grab them, and it frightened them almost out of their senses. They questioned for the hundredth time where their parents could be, and what was going to happen to them. It was long after midnight when the kindly leaves above their heads lulled them into slumber and for a time they forgot their sorrows in blessed sleep.

*Look! Lucretia Ann! Look at that bad
girl! Did you ever see the beat of what
she's done? Look!*

CHAPTER NINE

LUCRETIA ANN woke next morning dreaming that Grandmother Pettigrew was frying hot cakes and calling:

"Wake up, little lazybones, and come to breakfast."

She thought she had started to pour thick maple syrup from the funny old Toby jug, and that the bright copper kettle which always stood on the kitchen shelf so dazzled her eyes that she could not see to pour. She blinked, and lay bewildered for a moment. Then she realized that the brightness was caused by the morning sun shining in her eyes from high in the heavens, and that it was indeed a long way from Grandmother Pettigrew's peaceful kitchen. Memory told her that she and Dimmis were alone on the desert with the Indians.

The small girl lifted herself slightly on one elbow, and gazed about, dreading what she might see. But a peaceful scene met her eyes. The men were nowhere in sight, and later she found that they had gone for an all-day fishing trip. The dark-skinned baby was rolling on the grass, and cooing to himself as contentedly as the small Faith might have cooed.

Dark Fawn, the child about their age, was playing on the white sands not far from where the girls were lying. She had made a wigwam, or wickiup, from a piece of skin, painted in gay design. Brightly colored pebbles were arranged in a semi-geometrical plan about the little tent, and leaves and flowers were stuck among them. An odd-looking doll, made from a bit of bone, was propped outside the wigwam. Dark Fawn was as much absorbed and interested in her play as the girls themselves might have been.

"Why, Indian children play just as we do!" Lucretia Ann thought in astonishment.

The squaw was squatted on a blanket sorting what the children later learned were colored porcupine quills, with which she embroidered her family's garments. The grandmother too was busy. She had gathered quantities of the slender willows which grew near by, stripped them of their bark, had them soaking, and with skilled fingers, wonderfully nimble in one of her age, was weaving a large, elaborate basket.

Still almost half asleep, the child gazed in wonder at the Indians. Why, this family was working together, just as she and Mother and Grandmother Pettigrew had worked. She had always thought of Indians as fierce savages, and had never imagined that they might have their pleasures, joys, and duties just as she had hers.

But now daydreams stopped and recollection flooded her mind. She sat up with a start and shook Dimmis saying excitedly:

"Wake up, Dimmis. Wake up quickly!"

Lucretia Ann herself hopped up quick as a wink, shook the wrinkles from the billowing folds of the beloved birthday dress, and stood poised a moment under the monstrous cottonwood tree, a vivid scarlet figure with the sun making her hair a golden cloud.

"My stars and garters, Dimmis," she cried anxiously, raising her hands palms outwards, as she unconsciously and comically imitated Grandmother Pettigrew in her most perturbed moments. "My stars and garters, aren't we the silliest things? Lying here like two lumps dreaming, when maybe our wagons passed hours ago. We were going to get up early and watch for dust, or for anyone passing by, and now look at us! Hurry quick, and we'll run across the river and see."

"Oh, do you think our folks could have passed? We were silly," agreed Dimmis, rubbing her sleepy eyes as she jumped to her feet and followed the little figure which led the way. Holding her scarlet skirts to her knees so that they should not get wet, Lucretia Ann paddled splash! splash! through the shallow part of the river, and then, balancing lightly, ran swiftly over the log which formed a bridge across the deeper part of the water. The children crowded through the dense thicket of willows bordering the river, and climbed to the top of a rocky mound which commanded a view of the plains through which the trail ran.

Only the lonesome waste, glistening in the sun, met their gaze.

There was no sign of dust to east or west to indicate that caravans of human beings had ever passed or would ever pass that way. Lucretia Ann sat down on the ridge with her hands clasping her knees, the picture of tired misery, and gazed into the distance. Dimmis stood beside her with hands interlaced above her eyes and looked and looked and looked as though she hoped to pierce through space and find some answer to her inward questions. Then she placed her arms about Lucretia Ann with a huge sigh.

"It seems as though everyone has forgotten us, doesn't it, Lucretia Ann?" she asked. "Well, we have each other, and maybe we can yet find Benjamin."

"That's true," said Lucretia Ann hopefully. "I'd forgotten about him for the moment. The men all seem to be away, even that horrid Big Mouth, so perhaps we can hunt for him. I am sure that if the nice grandmother knows she will tell us, if we can make her understand. Let's try. We'll make signs, if words don't do."

Back to camp they raced, with curious Dark Fawn at their heels. She had followed them part way across the river, and had been peering at them from the bushes. The grandmother approached with two bowls of a strong-smelling meat stew, and a basket of huckleberries.

"We'd better eat before we ask about Benjamin," said Lucretia Ann. "My, I don't like the smell of that stew!" The berries they enjoyed, and tried not to make wry faces at the taste of the meat. When they had finished what they could eat, Lucretia Ann knelt beside the grandmother, who had resumed her weaving.

"Couldn't you tell me where my kitty is?" she pleaded in her most coaxing manner, patting the grandmother's arm. "Where did that boy put him, and is he being good to him? He'll be lonely without me, because I've had him ever since he was a teeny-weeny baby, just so long, that I could hold in my hands like a ball of fur. I want him so much. Can't you help me find my kitty?"

The grandmother, of course, could not understand a word. Dimmis tried her hand.

"Listen, Grandmother, this is what we want— meow—meow—meow—" she repeated over and over, at the same time stroking an imaginary kitten.

The grandmother looked puzzled, but Dark Fawn laughed—a rather harsh, disagreeable laugh.

"She wants her animal. I think brother hid him away in a cave," she explained to the old lady.

The wrinkled face lighted with understanding, and the old squaw spoke to both the child and the other squaw, plainly asking if they knew where the cat had been hidden. Both shook their heads in denial, and if they knew refused to tell. The grandmother, indeed, searched and led them up and down near the camp, but they hunted in vain.

"Perhaps our mothers are hunting us just the way we are looking for our Benjamin," said Lucretia Ann sadly.

"I am sure they are, only harder," comforted Dimmis.

Dark Fawn now made shy advances toward the girls, showing that she wanted to play. While all three were standing looking at one another a loud chattering overhead attracted the Indian girl. She rushed quietly to the wickiup, and returned with her miniature bow and arrow. "Spang" whizzed the arrow, but the loud-chattering, saucy bird had flown away before the arrow reached its mark, much to the child's disgust.

However, she chose for a target a blazed spot on one of the trees, and both Dimmis and Lucretia Ann were amazed at the trueness of her aim. Each had played with her brother's bows and arrows at home, and felt that perhaps she might compete with the dark-skinned child. But, though they shot again and again, their arrows fell wide of the mark. Dark Fawn was not a polite hostess —she laughed in glee to think that she was more skillful than her guests, and strutted shamefully. But the children did not mind.

"You just wait until I tell Brother Tom how that little Indian girl can shoot. She can beat him all to nothing," Lucretia Ann cried.

Dark Fawn now led the way to the river side, where her little wickiup was standing. The girls examined everything, and especially the funny bone doll, with deep interest. When Dark Fawn saw that, she grabbed the doll, and ran like the wind to the grandmother, returning just as swiftly without her child.

"Let's show her how we build our houses," suggested Dimmis. So the three sat on the sands, and played happily together, Dimmis and Lucretia Ann with little pieces of bark and driftwood trying to make a house much like those in New England to show Dark Fawn. They made orchards, flower gardens, and hedges, and passed a happy

151

morning recalling the old homes, in spite of their anxiety.

About noon the grandmother came down to the river with a basket and some oddly shaped pointed sticks in her hands. From the basket she drew two little bone dolls, and gave them to the girls, smiling kindly at their delight, and then motioned for all three to follow her. She led the way to a barren, rocky little hill, and began busily digging with her stick. Dark Fawn dug too, and they brought up small, fleshy, onion-shaped roots. The girls watched with interest for a few minutes, and then Lucretia Ann said:

"Let's try and see if we can dig some too. I can tell now the kind of leaf they have. Perhaps the grandmother will give us a stick."

Digging in the hard, rocky earth was none too easy, but they managed to twist some of the roots from the soil. They were a variety of the camas or Indian potato, which the Indians use in large quantities for food.

Following Dark Fawn's example, the girls tried eating the raw bulbs, but found them tasteless and pasty.

"Ugh!" said Dimmis making a face. "These Indians do eat the funniest food! How can they like these things?"

"Maybe they cook them. Anyway, I expect

they would think our foods funny. See, the grandmother and Dark Fawn are gathering so many.
Gracious me! aren't they thick in this little valley?"—for just over the hill was a low meadow
where bulbs grew in great quantity.

When the basket was almost full they all returned to camp, and the bulbs were handed to the
younger squaw who prepared them for eating.
Some she dropped into a lined basket in which she
had made boiling water by throwing in hot stones;

these were boiled like potatoes, and the children were hungry enough to eat a few. The rest were prepared in a curious manner. The squaw placed them in a deep, wide hole, which had been lined with stones, among which a very hot fire had been built. When the rocks were very warm, the fire was raked out, the bulbs placed in this oven in a nest of thick grass, and the whole covered with earth.

"Whatever do you think she can be making?" asked Lucretia Ann.

"Maybe she's baking those things in an outdoor oven the way we bake potatoes when we go camping," suggested Dimmis.

She was right. The bulbs were left to cook overnight, and when the oven was opened in the morning they formed a thick, sweetish mass, which the Indians thought delicious.

Later, the grandmother returned to her weaving, while the girls sat by and watched her with interest. The basket seemed wonderful to them, and indeed it truly was a beautiful piece of workmanship. Dimmis took up several pieces of the willow which the squaw had discarded, and folded them idly in her hands, wondering if in all her life she could make anything as clever as this old, shriveled Indian was doing. The grandmother, seeing this interest, gave each child, as well as her red-skinned granddaughter, some long slender reeds, and patiently showed them how to start a most simple basket. At the same time she directed Dark Fawn to help them. She was already quite skilled in weaving, and was pleased to be allowed to help the palefaces, though she laughed at their clumsy efforts. In a short time each child was drawing the supple willows in and out, in and out, and feeling very proud of her efforts.

"Won't Mother be s'prised when she sees what we've learned to make? Why, we can weave baskets for everyone. Maybe I can make one to send to Grandmother Pettigrew, and perhaps I can make Mother a clothesbasket. She had to leave hers behind," said Lucretia Ann enthusiastically.

"Maybe," said Dimmis, smiling to herself at the idea of Lucretia Ann making a clothesbasket, for she well knew how eager her friend was to try new things, and how quickly she tired of doing them.

Not once was the trail forgotten, for the children hoped that soon their parents, or someone who would take them to their parents, would pass this way. They chose for their work a place near the grandmother where there was a slight clearing in the trees, through which they could watch the road, which was somewhat higher than the river. Every little while one of them would scamper across the stream and, perched on top of their sentinel rock, look searchingly to the east and the west. It was strange that no wagons seemed to be passing, for on many days the trail was a succession of travelers.

The sun was now high in the heavens and brought such heat that the children lost all heart for work. Finally Dark Fawn put her basket aside, and started on a run, beckoning the girls to follow. They saw her slip from her tunic and plunge into the river, laughing and daring them to do likewise.

"Shall we?" asked Lucretia Ann.

"Why not?" replied Dimmis. "It's terribly hot, and we can watch the road, even if we are in the river. I'd like a bath, for we surely are dirty. If anyone comes we can slip into our clothes in a jiffy."

The river was shallow on this side, and the sand so clean, white and alluring, that the girls hesitated no longer. The water had been heated enough by the sun to make it delightfully refreshing. It was fun, too, to watch this dark-skinned mermaid who was so much at home in the water. Once she dived into a long, deep, dark pool, and was under until the children feared she had been drowned. They were just ready to start up the bank screaming for help, when they saw her climbing out yards away, ready to jump in again. Sometimes she floated quietly with the current, like a bronze statue with long black hair streaming out behind. She swam under and above the water like a darting fish. Once she dived down quickly and came up with a small, wiggling fish in her hands, which she proceeded calmly to eat, laughing at the girls' looks of shocked surprise.

"I'm sick of watching her when she does such things as that," said Lucretia Ann. "Let's have a water frolic."

Splashing the water about each other, they entirely forgot Dark Fawn. Lucretia Ann had just fallen down under a shower of water thrown by Dimmis, and had gotten up laughing, preparing to return the sprinkling, when she saw Dimmis' body stiffen, and her face grow angry and shocked.

"Look, Lucretia Ann. Look at that bad girl. Did you ever see the beat of what she has done! Look!"

Lucretia Ann looked. She gave a cry and went rushing from the river.

"She shan't have it," she cried. "She shan't have it. I'll fight her. That's my own beautiful birthday dress, and I won't let her have it."

It's no wonder that she was angry, for Dark Fawn had taken the birthday dress and the scarlet

157

stockings, put them on, and was strutting about with great glee. She heard Lucretia Ann's cry, and started to run, but first she stopped to grab the morocco-topped shoes, which had been too small for her to wear. Lucretia Ann was so swift in bounding from the river that she overtook Dark Fawn and tried to tear the dress from her. The Indian mother, hearing the tumult, started towards the girls, but before she reached them, Dark Fawn broke from Lucretia Ann's grasp and bounded swiftly as one of the desert rabbits off among the trees. The mother gave a grunt and a laugh, picked up her child's discarded clothing, handed them to Lucretia Ann with what seemed like a harsh command to put them on, and then, shrugging her shoulders and laughing she marched away.

"I'll never, never wear those smelly, dirty things," she cried. "Never! I'll run around in my underwear or anything. Oh, I wish I could be with my dear Grandmother Pettigrew now." She sat there in a pitiful little heap, sobbing loudly.

Dimmis slowly dressed, and then stood there sorrowfully watching her friend. She longed so to comfort her, but what was there to say? What Lucretia Ann would finally have done will not be known, for Dimmis looked down the trail and shouted with all her might:

"Dust! Dust! Somebody's coming up the trail. Put on some clothes, Lucretia Ann. Anything, it doesn't matter what. Hurry, I'll help you."

Lucretia Ann slipped on some of her own garments, put the moccasins which Dark Fawn had left on her feet, and as she ran pulled the dirty fringed buckskin tunic over her head. An odd little figure she made, for the tunic was very short and showed her dimpled knees in what Mother would have thought a most improper manner. Little she cared how she looked.

"Let's run, whoever it is, and not wait to see," she panted to Dimmis. "If we find it's Indians we can turn and run back again. And, oh, Dimmis, pray, pray that it is our fathers."

So the girls threw all caution aside, crossed the river, fought their way through the willows, and began winding about the tall sage. Over the top of the brush they could finally see what had caused the dust. It was no caravan, but merely three horsemen. The girls recognized them as Lucretia Ann's brother Stephen, and Mr. Greene from the caravan. The third man they later learned was a government scout. They were trotting along at a brisk pace and were almost abreast of the children by the time they had crossed the river. A slight wind blew the dust to the far side of the riders so that the girls could see them plainly.

"Scream! Yell, Dimmis, as loud as you can. Holloa, Stephen! Mr. Greene! Holloa! Stop! Wait!"

But the voices did not carry far enough to reach the speeding horses, whose riders thought they were keeping such a sharp lookout. The Indian camp was securely hidden among the trees, and Stephen could not dream that his little sister was almost within a stone's throw of him, running her little heart out as she darted in and out among the obscuring sage, which threw out long, clawlike fingers to impede her progress.

"Brother Stephen, wait for me! Mr. Greene, we're coming! Wait, w-a-i-t!"

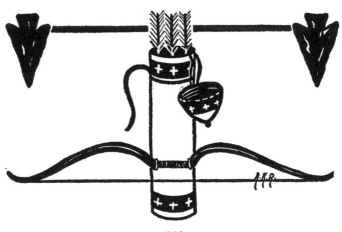

Oh, why did not that hurrying cloud of dust, which seemed to be ever following, gather the words and fling them into Stephen's ears, telling him to hasten back and enfold his lost sister in his arms?

By the time the girls had reached the road, the figures were becoming smaller with the distance, and soon they were mere specks which were shrouded in a cloud of dust, and faded entirely away.

Oh!   Lucretia Ann!   Would you dare?
All alone in the dark?

CHAPTER TEN

THE children followed the riders for awhile. Then, realizing that it was useless to run any farther, they sat flat in the middle of the road to ponder the unbelievable thing which had happened. Dimmis' face was one wrinkle of anxiety, but Lucretia Ann was angry clear through.

"Here I sit in this terrible old smelly Indian leather dress," she cried, "and my own brother rides by and does not see me! Where is everybody else, I'd like to know, and don't they care for us any more at all?" Her feet made the dust fly, and she wailed loudly, not caring how badly she was acting. Dimmis tried to comfort her. If her stout-hearted little chum lost heart, whatever should she do?

"Don't, Lucretia Ann," she begged. "Please don't scream so loud. If we sit by the road and wait, maybe the rest of the caravan will come. You know some of the men and boys often ride ahead on horseback, and maybe we'll see the folks in an hour or two. Wipe your eyes, honey, and let's get in the shade of a sagebrush and wait."

So the two sat in the doubtful shade of a giant sage, and waited and waited and waited. Once, several Indians rode by, and again several rough-

165

looking whites. The children saw them in the distance and were frightened at their wild looks, so they hid breathless in the sagebrush as they trotted by. The sun sank lower and lower, and Lucretia Ann finally said:

"It's no use, Dimmis. You know the folks camp long before the sun gets this low. See, it's getting dark. I guess there's nothing to do but go back to camp."

So the children retraced their steps, and on the way they met the kind old Indian grandmother hunting through the sage. Her bent form was hobbling here and there as she peered about, and her nearsighted eyes lighted with relief when she saw the children. She had looked on with disapproval when the fluttery scarlet dress was taken, and in Indian fashion had brought something to replace the loss. She slipped some strands of bright beads about Lucretia Ann's neck, and handed her a pair of beautifully beaded moccasins. To Dimmis she gave a water bottle, woven with gay figures. Lucretia Ann for a moment lay her head against the grandmother's arm. It seemed sweet to know that at least one friendly heart was near. Then the girls followed her back toward the camp, their heads drooping despairingly, and their unwilling feet scraping up the dust. By the clamor and confusion they knew that something had happened during their absence. The men had returned from a successful fishing trip—they had been spearing the fish, and held up two of monstrous size for the old squaw to see; a third had already been cut up, and the girls saw Dark Fawn sitting stolidly in the scarlet dress eating a huge chunk raw.

"Dimmis, can those be fish?" queried Lucretia Ann. "Why, they're almost as long as we are."

"They must be fish, for they look like them.

Lucretia Ann, they make me think of the talking fish in my book of fables. Don't you remember how the genie sent them out of the sea to work evil magic? Oh, look, Lucretia Ann. They're eating them raw."

It was true. They were eating greedily of the raw fish, and one of the Indians smilingly handed each girl a great chunk. The children curtsied and smiled, and Lucretia Ann said in her prettiest manner:

"Oh, thank you. Thank you very much," which delighted the man, who liked to hear them talk.

"O Lucretia Ann, I can hardly bear to touch this. It makes me feel sick, it's so raw and slick."

"It does look awful, Dimmis," agreed Lucretia Ann, "but you know how good baked fish is, and I'm as hungry as a bear. We haven't eaten a decent meal since yesterday morning, and I was too full from the day before to eat very much then."

"I'm hungry too," said Dimmis. "Maybe if we take this to the river and wash it well, we can try and cook some. If the grandmother will let us have her knife we can cut off some pieces and put them on sticks and try and toast them over the fire just as we used to roast apples and potatoes when we played house."

There was a roaring fire, for the Indians were preparing to cook and dry the fish; they were roasting great chunks of it, and some was being cooked in clay-lined baskets filled with cold water, into which the squaws dropped red-hot rocks to make the water boil. The children managed to haggle off some pieces of the fish, and were partially successful in their efforts to roast it. Some of the pieces caught fire; some were underdone, and some far too well cooked. They at last cooked some so it could be eaten, and the grandmother helped them out. When she saw what they were doing she stopped her own work, and wrapped some of the children's fish in a certain kind of green leaves. She placed these on heated rocks heaped with coals and ashes, and before long the girls had really excellent roast fish. This, with fresh huckleberries, made a most satisfying meal. They felt less lonely and forlorn now that they were not hungry.

Later the two leaned against the trunk of a huge cottonwood tree, and watched the scene about the fire with fascinated eyes. The men were lounging about joking and laughing, and the glowing coals lighted their bright-hued blankets, bronzed faces, and coal black hair which fell about their shoulders. Years afterwards, when Lucretia Ann was lying in the dark, that vivid picture would often pass before her eyes. The oldest Indian was telling some wonderful tale, and the children were laughing at the comical sound of a strange tongue, and the odd gestures. All at once Lucretia Ann jumped to her feet.

"Come with me; hurry fast," she whispered as she pulled Dimmis along.

In through the willows she dashed, up the bank of the river, and down through a grassy little meadow, with Dimmis wondering and panting at her heels.

"Where are you going, Lucretia Ann?" she gasped. "And why are you running so fast? I cannot keep up with you."

"Hush," was the reply. "Run quietly. Don't make a speck of noise."

For several minutes the puzzled Dimmis followed Lucretia Ann in and out among the bushes, pausing when she paused, crouching low to listen when her friend crouched, and watching her as she gazed intently all around. Then the running stopped and Lucretia Ann said dejectedly:

"It's no use, Dimmis. I cannot follow. I know he threw me off the track on purpose. I saw that bad Big Mouth take a piece of fish and look to see if I was watching. He slid into the bushes just as if he did not want me to see, but I did. I think perhaps he has my kitty hidden some place and is going to feed him. Well, wherever he's gone I cannot tell, but he's gotten away. Let's hurry back. I'm scared among these dark bushes, aren't you?"

"I am. I'm scared all the time these days. I wish I knew where that nice little cat is. He would be such company for us."

"If I could have him in my arms I'd be so happy," sighed Lucretia Ann. "Anyway, let's crawl into bed. I do not want to watch these old Indians who have taken my dress and my kitty."

The children crawled wearily into the blankets under the friendly tree, and tried to forget their loneliness in sleep. But the ground was hard, the blankets smelly, and neither could rest well. Lucretia Ann thought of the soft, sweet-smelling bed upon which she and Mother slept while on the journey. Father wanted them to be as comfortable as possible, so he had fixed a light spring wagon. In the bottom of this wagon were placed all the trunks and boxes which need not be opened during the trip. On these were boards, then springs, a feather bed, and much of the bedding which was not in use and must be stored some place. Mother made the bed up freshly each week with sheets which smelled of lavender and rosemary, for even on the journey she kept bags of sweet herbs and leaves tucked among her linens.

The homesick child thought too of the pleasant evenings round the campfire. Travel stopped early so that there might be plenty of food and rest for the horses and oxen. When supper was cleared away, and the chores done there were visiting and laughter and fun. The children played games, romped and frolicked. Sometimes one group of caravaners entertained another. On rainy evenings there would often be a concert or program in one of the larger tents. The very last time there had been an entertainment both she and Dimmis had spoken pieces. When Lucretia Ann had been applauded she had gone back at Stephen's bidding, and spoken a little piece which he had taught her:

This world is round, just like a ball
It goes around and round.
I think if it should catch a fall
'Twould fall upon the ground.

Inside the circle of wagons drawn up for protection and safety was a gathering of folks like one big, friendly family. Lucretia Ann finally fell asleep wondering what this big family was doing tonight.

The next day the children spent in very much the same manner that they had spent the previous one. Part of the time they watched the squaws, who busied themselves with various household tasks, for the men had again gone fishing. They worked drying the fish, gathering some shriveled berries which grew along the riverbank, and from the rocky hillside dug quantities of the camas, of which they all seemed very fond. Dark Fawn followed them about, every bit as proud of the birthday dress as its owner had been. She strutted so proudly, smoothing her scarlet ruffles, that the girls could hardly stand it. It was too tight, and when Lucretia Ann noticed that she had split out many of the carefully worked buttonholes, she burst into tears, for Grandmother Pettigrew made the most perfect buttonholes of anyone in the whole neighborhood, and was more than proud of her skill.

"Dimmis," said Lucretia Ann, with teardrops rolling down her cheeks, "my grandmother always makes excuses for people. She just chuckles and says: 'That's all right. Life's too short to let a little thing like that make us unhappy, isn't it?' But I don't think she'd laugh if she saw my pretty birthday dress on that ugly Indian, and me in these filthy skins."

"No, she wouldn't laugh," agreed Dimmis soberly, "but I know what she would do. She would think of something to say to cheer us up, just the same."

Weaving the baskets which they had started proved interesting work. Much of the day the girls sat where they could watch the trail, as they drew the damp willow strands in and out. The grandmother had chosen a simple pattern, and was most patient about her teaching. Before night, each had her basket finished.

It was well that their fingers could be busy, for the girls found waiting this day harder than before. Everyone in camp seemed restless. Time and again the Indian squaws looked anxiously towards the trail, and several times they wandered up and gazed into the distance down its rutted length. The children could feel that they were the subject of much speech between the two.

"They're jabbering about us, Lucretia Ann," said Dimmis. "They're wondering where our folks are, I guess, and they don't know what to do with us."

"I see them looking at us often. Perhaps they don't want us any more than we want them. Oh, why don't our fathers come and hunt us?"

Night again fell, and with it the return of the men with more fish. The girls went to bed early, but not to sleep. From indications of packing, they felt almost sure that the Indians planned to be on the move tomorrow—where, of course, they could not guess. Perhaps they would again take the trail into unknown parts, so far away that they would never be found. Why, why did no one seem to be hunting them?

The camp finally grew silent. The wind whispered among the willows, and the river flowed softly so as not to awaken the sleeping flowers along its bank. Millions of stars twinkled happily in the sky. Lucretia Ann often loved to watch these stars, for she thought they looked like eager little children holding a dancing party far above the clouds. A beautiful night for dreaming, but the sorrowful child was too full of her wrongs and griefs to think of happy things. The stolen kitty, the stolen dress, the dirt, the smells, the dreadful things the Indians ate all seemed to her personal injuries. An overwhelming wave of homesickness overcame her. She could, and would stand it no longer. Even the barren desert seemed preferable to these strange people. She shook Dimmis, who was falling asleep.

"Dimmis," she whispered, "I know what we'd better do. We'd better run away. Maybe the Indians would let us go, anyway, and maybe they wouldn't. I am sure that's the Oregon Trail, and we know Stephen and the other men have gone that way. Father told me that last morning that we were only a few days' journey from the trading post, for he promised to buy me some sticks of hoarhound candy when we got there. We can take our salmon and the water jug and follow the trail. Surely some wagons will come by tomorrow, and we can ride to the post. Almost all the time there have been wagons either ahead of us or behind us. If our folks aren't there we can wait. Anyone would be kind enough to keep two little girls."

"O Lucretia Ann, would you dare?" Gentle Dimmis was almost stunned with the thought of such an adventure.

"Well, I would dare just as much as I would dare to stay here. I don't like it, and I am afraid these Indians will pack up and take us some place where we will never see our parents again."

"But *Lucretia Ann! All alone in the dark!* Could we?"

"Don't you ever want to see your mother or

your father or your darling little sister Faith again?" scolded Lucretia Ann angrily. "Do you want to stay with these Indians forever and eat raw fish and chew skins to make your clothes, and be a little savage girl?"

"I do not! I do not! I will go with you and do whatever you say. Truly I will."

The kind old man in the moon shed his softest, mellowest light upon the two tiny girls trudging along alone so bravely.

CHAPTER ELEVEN

"WELL, then, we'd better go tonight just as soon as we think everyone is asleep. I hate to leave my kitty, but sometimes I'm afraid he's been eaten in a stew. That's why I couldn't even look at the meat they gave me.

"I'll tell you what we must do. We must lie here quietly, and don't you dare to shut your eyes. I won't either. When we are sure that everyone is asleep I will crawl out and get our salmon. It is packed in our baskets near the grandmother's bed. Then we must creep softly across the river so that not even a twig will snap."

Dimmis was becoming as excited as Lucretia Ann.

"Yes, and if we walk all night we can go a long way. Perhaps we'll find a caravan camping ahead. We must be sure to drink lots of water before we leave the river because our jug does not hold very much. O Lucretia Ann, let's hurry and get away."

A while longer they whispered and planned, waiting for the camp to grow quiet. Then, how still everything was! How dark! How scary! How spooky it sounded in the shadows! And how very tired they were!

A soft breeze was teaching a lullaby to the

rustling cottonwood trees above them, and in a few minutes both children were sound asleep. They probably would have slept until morning, but in an hour or two softly padded footsteps came creeping through the camp. A tiny figure darted in and out among the shadows; there was a gentle bur-r-r-, bur-r-r-, and Lucretia Ann was awakened by her own dear Benjamin who had escaped from the cave in which Big Mouth had hidden him, and was licking and nipping at her neck as he gave soft purrs of joy.

"O my baby Benjamin! My kitty! My kitty! Now we will surely go before they get you again," she whispered. "How did you get here, and weren't you the smart kitty to wait until everyone was asleep? You came just in time. Dimmis, Dimmis," she whispered, "wake and see who's here."

"Is it my mother?" murmured Dimmis drowsily.

"No, but see, Dimmis," and she placed the soft fur against her chum's cheek.

"Lucretia Ann, I shan't be half as scared to go with Benjamin along, will you?" she whispered joyfully. "Oh, let me hug him awhile."

"Yes, you hold him tightly, for I do not want him ever to get away again. I am sure everyone is asleep, and I am going to slip out and see if I can find the baskets."

Luckily the girls, after toasting and baking the fish which had been given them, had tucked all they had left in their baskets for future eating, covered it with many leaves, and hidden it under a bundle of skins so that one of the several dogs which were in camp might not make away with it.

"Your water jug is near there, too. My, I hate to go! I'm glad the moon is rising."

"Do, do, go carefully, Lucretia Ann," pleaded Dimmis.

Lucretia Ann raised herself carefully, and tiptoed softly, step by step, toward the pile of skins. She hardly dared breathe. Her heart was pounding so that she feared the Indians would hear it. There! she was just within reach of the baskets; she reached down to get them. In trying to be cautious she stubbed her toe, and fell headlong with her hands on the grandmother's blanket.

The old squaw was on her feet in a moment, alarmed at the crash and jar.

"Ugh! Ugh!" she grunted, roughly grasping the terrified child by the arm. Lucretia Ann felt that she could never live through such fright. What would be done with her for creeping about the camp at night as though she were bent on mischief? She need not have been frightened, however, for when the old woman saw that the intruder was only a trembling little girl, she evidently thought her lonely or afraid. She patted her kindly, and led her back to the blanket under the tree where Dimmis was lying. Dimmis, who had been almost as horrified as Lucretia Ann, hastily tucked Benjamin under her full skirts, and closed her eyes, as though asleep. The grandmother put Lucretia Ann beside her friend, and sat there a few moments, as though to still her alarm. The small girl gave the kind old hand a farewell pat, thinking how she hated to venture forth into the darkness with no one to turn to, no matter what might happen.

Again the girls lay quiet for a long, long time, not daring even to whisper. Then Lucretia Ann crept forth, this time on her hands and knees. She reached the baskets and the jug, and returned to the cottonwood tree. With a basket in one hand, and Benjamin tucked under her other arm, she led the way toward the river. Dimmis followed with her basket of fish and the water jug. They reached the river and filled the jug, both drinking, as Dimmis had suggested, large draughts of the water. As they started across, Dimmis' foot slipped, and there was a sharp clatter of stones. A dog started to bark; another, and then another. Would the whole camp be roused?

"Hide in the willows quickly," whispered Lucretia Ann. There they huddled together, the moonlight turning them into frightened little grey ghosts. At length the barking ceased, but they cautiously remained motionless some moments before venturing to cross the stream. Step by step they advanced; they gained the opposite bank in safety. Then how they ran! Lightly, silently, swiftly winding in and out about the silvered sage, until they reached the rutted trail. Then they still ran until every drop of breath seemed squeezed from their lungs. They crept in the shadow of a tall spreading sage, and listened for pursuing steps. All was silent. The Indians had evidently slept through their leaving, or it might be that they were glad to have them creep away.

The girls had begun to breathe calmly when over their heads they heard a harsh, fierce call. They grasped one another, too scared to move. There was no use in running, anyway; the pursuer was too close. Benjamin, however, was not so easily cowed. He let forth a frantic yowl, jumped from Lucretia Ann's arms, and sprang into the air. There was another harsh call, a fluttering of wings, and from the branch of a near-by dead sagebrush a horned owl flew into the sky.

"Only a bird!" Lucretia Ann laughed hysterically. "I thought it was an Indian giving a war whoop, and I thought I should die of fright, didn't you, Dimmis?"

"Well, I think I should have if Benjamin had not helped us out. Benjamin, come here and let me give you a bit of fish for being so good."

Again they took the trail. The kind old man in the moon looked down and smiled. He had seen thousands of sights on this trail, but never one which touched him more than the two tiny girls trudging along so bravely. The one, holding her curly head so valiantly was carrying a tortoise-shell cat, while the other trudged trustingly and sturdily a step or two behind. He shed his softest, mellowest light upon them, and somehow, without knowing why, the children felt comforted. It seemed as though someone had kissed them with a gentle benediction.

On and on and on they trudged, until Dimmis stopped and clutched Lucretia Ann's arm.

"Look," she breathed, pointing to the brush. The moonbeams fell brightly on a little pointed white face, peering from out the darkened shadows. It stared unblinkingly. The girls, round-eyed, stared back.

"Is it an elf or a pixie or a fairy or what?" questioned Lucretia Ann. The slight whisper caused the figure to move, then turn like a flash and vanish into the desert. The girls now knew

they had been startled by a monstrous grey jack-rabbit, which had peered at them inquiringly from the brush. Benjamin saw him too and felt that he had had enough of being carried, and that this was an opportunity for a good chase. In the twinkling of an eye he was on the ground, and the black darkness, like a hungry ogre, had swallowed him.

"Now he's gone, and that is the last straw," said Lucretia Ann despairingly. She did not cry; she did not lament. She sat quietly down by the edge of the trail, put her chin in the palm of her hand, and gazed dejectedly into the darkness, as though her courage had vanished with the cat. Dimmis came to the rescue.

"He's just having a little fun. He'll come back." But though they called and called, and pleaded, and begged, their voices seemed to fall on deaf sage. For perhaps half an hour they sat there, and then Dimmis began to sob:

"I'm afraid. Even a little cat is a lot of company. The desert is a terrible place to be. O my mother, my mother, my mother."

The girls cried awhile together, cuddled in one another's arms. Then Lucretia Ann decided:

"Well, my kitty does nothing but cause me trouble. It's a dreadful thing to do, but we must go on and leave him. We must make for the post just as fast as we can before we get out of food and water. And the Indians might decide to come after us, and I don't want to be with them again. Come, Dimmis, let us go."

She started to rise, and felt a prickling, pulling tug on her arm. There was naughty Benjamin starting to purr, and looking at his delighted mistress with twinkling eyes, as though he knew he were giving her a lovely surprise.

"O you dear kitty. No matter how cross I get,

I am always so happy when I see you. Now we must hurry ahead. Come here, you rascal."

More tramping. Then Lucretia Ann said:

"I cannot carry this cat any longer. He is too heavy, and he wants to get down. But if I let him down he will run away." She stood panting for breath.

Then Dimmis laughed.

"I know what we'll do, Lucretia Ann. He just loves this fish, and we'll bribe him to walk. We'll give him a tiny bit of fish, and carry some more in our hands. He will smell it and want more, and will follow. Every little while we can give him a taste."

Benjamin ate the wee bit with great satisfaction, and Dimmis' scheme worked beautifully. The cat followed, and though at times he sank deep into the dust, he lifted his stout little legs and trudged cheerfully on, now and then giving a yowl for more fish as he sniffed eagerly at the baskets.

"He'll not leave us now," said Dimmis.

It seemed as if there was no end to the terrors of that night. Every leaf that rustled, every faint stir caused the friends to start and grasp one another apprehensively. A slight breeze arose toward dawn, which was accompanied by an occasional puff of wind. From the west, coming down the trail to meet them, the children saw what looked like a group of figures advancing rapidly, leaping, running, prancing. They again crouched terrified in the bushes, and only when the figures came very near did the children see that they were not running Indians, but merely immense tumbleweeds, which needed only a puff of wind to send them frisking and dancing merrily over the desert.

"O Dimmis," gasped Lucretia Ann in great relief, "if we weren't such cowards, we wouldn't expect everything to be so much worse than it is. Let's be more brave after this. See how lovely the moon is. It almost looks sorry for us."

"Yes, and see! There is a little pink in the sky. Morning cannot be far off, and then we will not be so afraid. I wonder how far we have walked. It seems to me to be about a hundred miles."

"Well, on to Oregon!" sighed Lucretia Ann.

Again they gathered their burdens and were on their way. And now came their last fright, which was the worst of all. A howl arose—a terrible, weird howl, which echoed over the desert, and was indeed the voice of the desert. There is nothing more mournful and lonesome than this long-drawn wail at which the children had often shuddered as they lay tucked in bed in the safety of the caravan.

They looked up. Straight at their right, on a small hillock, a large coyote stood sharply silhouetted against the sky. His nose was pointed toward the moon, as he gave forth piercing cries, which were caught and thrown back by answering coyote voices.

"Now is the time to take to our heels, Dimmis. That old thing hasn't seen us yet, but he will. Run! Run! Run for your life!"

"Yes, we'd better crouch low among the bushes so he can't see us. And run, run as we've never run before!"

Run they did. It seemed as though their tired little heels had wings. Stumbling, falling in their haste, with the sharp branches of the brush catching, tearing, hindering, they ran until the noise had receded into the distance, and they felt that they might rest in safety.

"I can't go another step, Lucretia Ann. Not another step," gasped Dimmis. "Not if I get eaten by the coyotes or captured by Indians. I'm not going to stir again."

"Well, I can't go any more, either. Let's just stop and rest until the sun rises. We can hunt a spot away from the road where the brush is thick. Let's hide there, where we can hear anyone who is going by, but where no one can see us unless we want them to."

"That is the thing to do."

A few rods away from the road was a tiny hollow. Immense buckbrush surrounded it; the brush was so thick that the top branches intertwined and formed a complete, hidden shelter. One could hide there and not be seen unless someone passed directly by. The girls crept into this and threw themselves wearily on the ground. They rested some moments, and then Dimmis said:

"I'm hungry, aren't you? And my mouth is dry as dust. I spilled part of the water when I fell, but we can drink some, can't we, and eat a little?"

"Let's," agreed Lucretia Ann. "We will feel better if we do. I did not know anyone could be so tired."

"Nor have so many troubles," groaned Dimmis.

The fish tasted good; the careful drinks of water better. The children fed Benjamin and let him drink from their hands. Then Lucretia Ann said, with her most motherly air:

"Put your head in my lap, Dimmis. You are so tired. I'll lean against this sagebrush and listen. Morning is almost here, but I do not think anyone will go by so early. I will watch while you sleep awhile, and then I will waken you, and you can watch while I rest."

Tired Dimmis was asleep in two minutes, cuddled as close to her chum as possible, for the night air was cool. Lucretia Ann gazed tenderly at the heart-shaped little face, framed with the heavy black braids falling over her shoulders. A pitiful little face it was, so streaked with dust mingled with tear drops, that her own mother would have found it hard to know her dainty daughter. She stroked the hair gently from her forehead, and drew in deep breaths of the spicy sage which the sweet morning breeze was bringing over the desert.

"I'll watch her. I'm stronger than she is. I wouldn't want anything to happen to my friend. I must keep hold of Benjamin with one hand too. Wouldn't it be fun if I should find her folks while she sleeps? I will stay awake. I—I—I—" Dear little Lucretia Ann's head bent lower and lower until it touched Dimmis' shoulders. She too was in the Land of Nod.

But not so Benjamin. He had had plenty of sleep during his long imprisonment in the cave. He wanted fun. He frolicked awhile with a funny small lizard which the girls' coming had dislodged. He frisked in and out among the bushes. He dragged the fish from each basket, ate what he pleased, and rolled the rest among the dirt and leaves. He knocked over the water jug, and was delighted at the little gurgles which issued from it as the precious fluid ran away. He lapped a little, and daintily slapped with his paw at the trickling stream which was greedily sucked up by the thirsty dust. Then he too became tired, and fell asleep with his mischievous head resting trustingly on his small mistress' sunburned, dirty arm.

Blow the bugle, Stephen. We must call a council.

CHAPTER TWELVE

A HAPPY caravan started from the river of green meadows that August day the children had their great adventure. The long rest, with plenty of cool water and fresh food had given new life and hopes to the tired party. Mrs. Greensleave cheerily said:

"Folks, just think! We have been on the journey more than three months. The hottest part of the summer is over, and we are all safe and sound. Surely we can stand a little more when *home* is at the end."

"Home, sweet home," shouted Tom, turning a series of handsprings, and the rest of the party joined in the chorus, singing lustily as they worked, and feeling that the new home was indeed very near.

Mr. Prence's wagons were among those at the front of the caravan, which was a great advantage, for the oxen and horses, plodding knee deep in the rutted roads, kicked up such dense clouds that those in the rear were almost stifled. On so hot a day those allotted to the front ranks were indeed fortunate.

The trumpet sounded—the signal for starting.

On to Oregon! On to Idaho! Everyone to his place.

"Wagons all ready?" inquired Mr. Prence. Then, as always mindful of the beloved daughter, he asked:

"Where is little Lucretia Ann? I declare, Mother, I sometimes wish she were not so friendly. I miss her when she is absent."

"Dimmis wished her to ride with them. They have a new game which they are playing."

"I would think they would prefer to ride at the head of the column this oppressive day. In fact, I think it would be better if we required Lucretia Ann to do so."

"Children do not mind these things as we older people do. I think they dread the monotony more than the heat. She and Dimmis are coming to eat dried-apple pie for lunch and ride with us this afternoon. But I will send Tom to hunt her if you wish."

"No, let her have her fun. The girls may have their hearts set on some play which I should spoil. This journey is hard enough at the best," smiled Father indulgently.

"Where is Dimmis?" Mr. Greensleave was asking at almost the same time, and his wife replied:

"She wanted Lucretia Ann to ride with her, but Mrs. Prence has some of her famous dried-apple pies for lunch, so I presume they decided to ride there. Lucretia Ann wished to share this treat with Dimmis. Isn't she the most generous little thing? It is fortunate that Dimmis has such pleasant company on the trip."

"I am glad they decided to ride in the Prence wagon, for they are at the head of the column. This bids fair to be our hottest day, and the heat seems to tire Dimmis very much. She looks thin and worn."

The bugle sounded. With singing, laughing, and cracking of whips and shouting at oxen the caravan moved joyfully on its way, unmindful of the fact that Lucretia Ann Prence and Dimmis Greensleave were at that moment far up the river-bank, sifting the sparkling sand through their hands and starting a little prison cell for Benjamin. How horrified all would have been had they dreamed of such a thing!

The same unbearable sultriness of which the girls had complained oppressed the travelers. Babies wailed, the children fretted, the horses and oxen drooped their heads, while the men plodding beside the wagons continually wiped the sweat from their dripping faces. Then, of course, the same wind laden with sand came swooping down upon them.

When the party could no longer see to travel

on account of the blinding dust, it drew to one side of the trail and camped as the Indians had done. So it was some time past the regular lunch hour before the storm had abated so that eating could be thought of. When the girls did not appear Mrs. Prence said:

"Thomas, run and call the children to lunch. They planned to eat dried-apple pie with us this noon. Tell them to hasten for we have but a few minutes to stay. The storm has delayed us too much already. Even if they have eaten lunch Father thinks it better for Lucretia Ann to ride with us and escape the dust. Tell her to come this minute."

In almost the twinkling of an eye Tom returned wide-eyed and frightened, with Mr. and Mrs. Greensleave following.

"Mother," he shouted, "the girls are not there! Mrs. Greensleave has not seen them since morning, and she thought they were with you."

"I never dreamed but that they were in your wagon," exclaimed Mrs. Greensleave. "I can't think why they would do such thing, except for the fact that we know everyone in the train so well, and they evidently thought we would not care if they changed their plans."

"Mother, you ought not to let Lucretia Ann frighten us like that," roared Tom, whose worry had made him cross. "I hope you spank her good when you find her. I'll bet she and Dimmis are in the Gibson wagon. They like to snoop around there, for Mrs. Gibson gives them so many lozenges."

"Hush," said Father. "This is no time to scold! We must hunt. Let us make a systematic round of the wagons."

"We couldn't by any chance have left them behind?" queried Mrs. Prence, aghast at such a terrible thought.

Lunch was forgotten, for a hasty survey of the camp proved that the children were certainly missing. The last person who remembered having seen them was little Peletiah Sparrow. He told of having watched as they chased Benjamin up the river and over the small hill until they were out of sight.

"That wretched cat! Why did I ever let my soft heart get the better of my common sense? I knew I should leave him behind," groaned Mr. Prence.

"Father, how could we have been so careless as to leave without being certain our little daughter was with us? Do not blame the cat. Blame our lack of caution. O Paul, can anything have happened?" mourned Mrs. Prence. "I cannot forgive myself for being so heedless."

"Now, Mother, don't be fretting," said Mr. Prence, his own brow wrinkled with anxiety. "We'll start back at once, and likely as not we'll find them trudging up the road to meet us. Lucretia Ann has an uncommon lot of sense for a girl her age, and Dimmis is a smart one too."

"I know, Father, I know. But think how easily they could have become confused in the storm. It would be so easy for them to lose their way when the dust was so thick, and be wandering in the sagebrush. That looks all alike and is very confusing. They may be exhausted with heat, thirst, and fright."

"Blow the bugle, Stephen," said Father. "We must call a council at once and decide what to do."

An anxious crowd gathered, for all loved the sunny, fly-away Lucretia Ann, and quiet, serious Dimmis. Plans were hastily made. A few of the men would stay with the caravan, which would camp where it was. The rest would journey back to the river, two riding along the trail, the others making a detour into the brush, all keeping a sharp lookout for Indians. Mrs. Prence and Mrs. Greensleave insisted on riding back with the others.

"We mothers might think of some place to hunt which the rest would miss. Or, if either is hurt

we shall be needed. We should go crazy doing
nothing, and thinking of all the things which
might have happened to those babies."

Everyone wanted to join in the hunt; those who
must stay felt it a hardship. Good old deacon
Tracy, the oldest member of the party, said, when
told that he must stay with the wagons: "Well,
then, if I may not go, I shall spend my time pray-
ing. God will hear my prayers and protect those
bairns," and they left him kneeling in the desert.

The storm had swept clean all traces of the

lost ones, and through the afternoon the party hunted, with not the faintest trace to reward their efforts. Toward evening Stephen, Tom, and others found on the riverbank the stone prison, a wee toy belonging to Lucretia Ann, the scattered plum pits, and the broken branches of the tree. They also found two bouquets of bright flowers which the girls had gathered and weighted down with pebbles at the edge of the river to keep them from washing away while their stems remained in the water.

The caravan returned to the river. There was no sleep that night. Brush fires burned for the searchers, in spite of danger from Indians. Throughout the next day the search continued. No one knew what to suggest, for so many things might have happened. Though no Indians had been seen for many a day, there was the chance that a wandering band had found the girls; the river could have claimed them, though it was so shallow there was little likelihood of their being drowned. The majority felt that they might have become confused, and still be wandering in the sagebrush. Tom did not think so. He felt sure that they had taken the trail, and were following it.

"Father," he insisted, "perhaps Lucretia Ann and Dimmis came back right after we left. When they found we were gone they would try to hurry and catch us. During that terrible storm we went quite a little way from the trail to get out of the road dust. Maybe they walked right past us down the trail, or maybe some other wagons, or some people on horseback were following us and picked them up. They, too, could have passed us and think they were still following. If it happens that my poor little sister and Dimmis are walking they may be almost dying of hunger and thirst. I think we should send someone ahead to look."

"It may be you are right, Son, and we must leave no stone unturned. At any rate, we are finding no trace here. The fort is only a few days distant by wagon travel, and if someone rides swiftly ahead, he can spread an alarm among whites and Indians which may give us some clues for the search. Our freshest horses should reach the post tomorrow."

All agreed that this was the wisest course, so Stephen, Mr. Greene, and a government scout who had come up with the party were chosen, and rode off at top speed early that morning after the girls had been lost, and as we have seen, passed the children who had seen them, and who scampered after them as fast as their small legs could carry them through the sage which hid them from sight. Meanwhile, those who remained by the river searched far and wide that day and night, and finally, in sorrowful council decided to take the trail again the following day. It seemed a terrible decision to make.

"If we could hope to gain anything by staying here we would stay for weeks," said the captain, "even though many of our provisions are running low. But it seems that, wherever those children are, it is not here. They have vanished as though snatched into the clouds."

"I do not see how I can possibly go on without my baby," mourned Mrs. Prence. "Always, after this, the West will be a terrible nightmare. To turn back and go east without her would be just as bad. Why, why was I so careless? And what can we gain by staying here?"

"There's always hope, Mother," comforted her husband, who looked old and haggard and ill. "Perhaps Tom is right, and we may yet find the girl safe and sound at the trading post. Any party who picked them up would reasonably judge us to be ahead, and so would keep on moving toward the fort."

Mrs. Greensleave flatly refused to leave.

"We will stay," said her husband, "and take up with another caravan. The families who came in last night are about worn out, and want a rest. They have agreed to wait here for us several days. If wife feels better to stay, she shall do so until she is ready to leave. Sometimes a mother's instinct tells her what is best to do."

So the caravan made a very early start, and as the horses and oxen had had days of rest with luxurious feed, they traveled until late into the night. Continual detours were made by horsemen into the desert, and the waste was scanned by dozens of anxious eyes, but if the country knew the secret it kept it well. At length, with great weariness the travelers made camp several miles from the spot where little Lucretia Ann and Dimmis were huddled together planning to run away.

It wasn't a rabbit—it was Benjamin!

CHAPTER THIRTEEN

THE campers slept for a few hours and were off at the first break of day. All the tips of the sagebrush were burnished gold, and the desert was a softened thing of wondrous beauty. A faint breeze brought invigorating breaths of the spicy sage.

But Mr. and Mrs. Prence could see no glory in the desert—it was a monster who had snatched away their dearest treasure.

"Why did we leave our comfortable home to come to this horrible place? We tempted fate when we did so, for everything was going smoothly and we were all happy," lamented Mrs. Prence.

Most of the time, however, they traveled in silence, questioning in their minds for the thousandth time where the children could be. They had gone several hours, and the Prence wagons were in the lead. Suddenly Mrs. Prence grasped her husband's arm and screamed excitedly:

"Stop, Paul, stop! What did I see? Tell me quickly!"

"Nothing, Mother, nothing, unless it was that miserable cottontail running across the road."

"It wasn't that. It wasn't."

211

"Don't get so wrought up. We have passed thousands of them," soothed Mr. Prence.

"But it wasn't a rabbit," insisted his wife, already scrambling from the half-stopped wagon. "It was Benjamin, our cat, as sure as I live."

Mrs. Prence was trembling so that she could hardly stand when her feet touched the ground.

"Mother, you have lost your mind completely," replied her husband. "That is absolutely out of reason," but his wife paid no attention.

"Paul, I'd know that cat in China by the way he switches his tail, and then takes that funny leap. You can't fool me about Benjamin." She followed through the sagebrush calling:

"Here, kitty, kitty, kitty. Come, Benjamin. Nice kitty. Come, Benjamin. Paul, come and help me hunt. I cannot stand this."

Again and again she called. No sound. No movement of the dry desert grass.

"You certainly were mistaken, Mother. There is no earthly chance that our cat could be alone here on the desert. We have seen no sign of life for hours."

"But I tell you I saw him. Tom, run back and ask all the teams to stop for a few minutes so that we can hunt undisturbed. The cat was running after something, and seemed in high spirits. Paul, you know how Benjamin loves to pretend he does not hear us when we call. He will generally come for you. Try and call him back."

Other members of the caravan had quickly gathered, leaving the conveyances behind, and the excited group silently and breathlessly waited while Mr. Prence coaxed gently:

"Here, pusser, pusser—pusser—. Come, Benjamin, old boy."

One could almost hear the beating of the listeners' hearts, as they strained eyes and ears towards the desert.

Silence.

In the distance the stamping of oxen and horses, the clanking of chains.

More calling. Silence.

Then there was a rustle of dry grass, a shaking of sagebrush branches, a faint, half-muffled meow, and Benjamin with a bound came running toward Mr. Prence, and laid a half-grown rabbit at his feet. After an exciting chase the cat had found a breakfast much to his liking, and came to Mr. Prence for the same praise he always received in former days when he had laid a mouse at his master's feet. At sight of him a loud shout arose from the waiting crowd. Mrs. Prence gathered the cat in her arms, sobbing hysterically, while Tom jumped up and down, unashamed of the tears that were streaming down his cheeks.

"It gives me hope. It gives me hope," said Mrs. Prence. "My baby may be near. See how well-fed the cat appears. Kitty, can you not tell us where to hunt? Did you leave Lucretia Ann behind? Or has something happened to her?"

Benjamin meowed loudly as though he wanted to speak. He seemed wild with joy at seeing old friends, and gave friendly little licks to Mrs. Prence's arm and neck as she cuddled him close. He was satisfied to lie there quietly while the caravaners gathered around.

"I told you to have faith," said Deacon Tracy. "If the cat is alive and well, surely the children are too. Maybe a caravan is not far ahead, and Benjamin has strayed away."

As there had been no signs of human life for miles, the mystery of the cat's sudden appearance was deep, and the question of what to do was as puzzling as ever. Search was made for tiny steps in the already well-tracked road, but none was found, for the children had been running back among the brush after the coyote scare. Benjamin had apparently had plenty to eat and to drink, which would not have been the case had he been wandering alone for days. No one knew what to think, or what to suggest doing. As far as the eye could reach there was only the grey sage. As far as the ear could hear was silence. Shouting, firing of guns, and blowing of bugle elicited no response. So the best plan seemed to be to push on toward the fort, keeping an even sharper lookout, and hoping that they might come up with some wagon from which the cat had strayed.

"Come, Mother, we had better start again," said Mr. Prence. "The finding of this cat puts new life into me, and I have great hopes that we may see the children ahead."

"O Paul, it seems as if I cannot leave this spot where I found Lucretia Ann's kitten. I feel as though I am leaving behind all hope of ever seeing her. Benjamin, why can you not tell us where your little mistress is? Did you leave her behind, or did she come with you? Paul, let us wait a little longer."

Her arms stretched toward her husband, and Benjamin slipped down and vanished into the brush.

"We must not lose the cat. We must find him at all costs. Here is another chase. I declare, that cat must be bewitched!"

Both Mr. and Mrs. Prence followed as quickly as possible through the heavy sage; they could catch glimpses of the cat's form weaving in and out. Finally, they saw him leaping and mewing in delight about a little gully surrounded by very high, thick buckbrush, filled in with lighter sage.

Mrs. Prence was ahead; her haste was checked, and she stepped back in alarm. She had seen the heavily beaded tip of a moccasin, and a buckskin sleeve protruding from the sage. With her hands on her lips to denote caution, she motioned her husband to stop.

"Paul," she whispered in fright, "I saw the tip of a moccasin peeping from that clump of sage. There's an Indian there—perhaps a dozen. Oh, do be cautious, Paul."

Mr. Prence returned to the caravan for reinforcements. A circle of men, with raised firearms, surrounded the hollow. In the stillness they could hear Benjamin, jumping and meowing.

"That's a sure sign Benjamin is pleased," thought Mr. Prence. "I think Martha was mistaken about the Indians." He stepped forth more boldly and peered down at the beaded leather. There was something else too—a long, black, tangled braid, and then the weary little face of Dimmis, cuddled trustfully on the buckskin tunic.

"Can Dimmis be here, and with an Indian?" he thought, unable to believe his eyes. He bent closer, and his heart almost stopped beating. He gave a mighty shout of joy.

"Mother! Mother! Tom! Tom! Everybody! Our baby is found—and Dimmis. The lost are here. O my precious Lucretia Ann."

He had recognized his own little daughter in
the dirty buckskin robe, with Dimmis pillowed on
her lap. He lifted Dimmis to Deacon Tracy's out-
stretched arms, and ran toward his wife with his

sleeping daughter. Men were slapping one another on the back, and shaking hands. Women were exclaiming, and rushing up to one another with tears rolling down their cheeks. Children were shouting and dancing for joy. Deacon Tracy called "Glory to God! Glory to God!" and the whole caravan joyfully joined in raising their voices to the skies.

The children were so exhausted that they did not rouse in spite of the commotion. Lucretia Ann opened her eyes, looked from her father to her mother with a drowsy smile, murmured: "Do not forget my kitty," and drifted off to peaceful sleep.

The dirty, scratched little faces, hands, and feet were tenderly bathed, and the children in fresh little white nightgowns were placed in bed in the back of the light spring wagon. All day long Mrs. Prence guarded them, as though she feared at any moment they might vanish from her sight. And the caravan plodded along with laughter and song in spite of the heat and the dust. Though the desert had lost its golden light, and was dull and drab, Mrs. Prence said:

"Paul, after all this desert is really lovely. Those purplish shadows across the sage make it beautiful; and I shall long for the spicy odor if I am ever away."

Her husband smiled. He well knew that when the heart is light, everything is rose-colored to the view.

Has anyone seen a beautiful tortoise-shell cat walking all alone down the Oregon Trail?

CHAPTER FOURTEEN

ALL day long the caravan crept happily along the trail, while the children slept peacefully in the jolty bed. Swiftest horses sped east and west to carry the joyful news to the Greensleave family and to Stephen. The girls were too exhausted to arouse when lunch time came, so the whole party had to curb its impatience to hear the story.

All day long people came riding or walking up to the wagon to ask:

"O Mrs. Prence, aren't those darling girls awake? I cannot wait to hear their story." Or, "Mrs. Prence, I have some very rich rabbit broth which would be nourishing for those poor, dear lambs—they look half starved." On and on through the day all sorts of delicacies were drawn from secret hiding places and brought for those same "poor, dear lambs" who had been captured by the Indians.

Evening, with its leaping campfires and refreshing meal, roused them, and Lucretia Ann and Dimmis sat on humble blanket thrones like two small princesses whose subjects hung upon their slightest word. Of course everyone wanted to hear the story of the adventure from beginning to

223

end, and to hear it again and again. With each telling the children felt a little more important as they listened to the exclamations of astonishment and admiration. People asked question after question. Tom and the other boys were openly envious. They felt that they had missed the chance of a lifetime. To think of living two whole days in an Indian camp! When Lucretia Ann related how Big Mouth had stolen her cat, and laughed at her efforts to find him, her brother doubled his fists and said:

"If I had been there, Sister, that mouth of his would have stretched farther than ever over his old red face!"

And when she told how Dark Fawn ran off with the scarlet dress he growled:

"I wish I could have been there, and pushed her so deep into the river that she could never crawl out."

Indeed, Lucretia Ann, always a favorite, and sweet little Dimmis seemed about to have their heads completely turned by this sudden popularity. They began to feel that they were heroines, as indeed they were, though bad little heroines, at that.

Hadn't they been captured by a band of Indians, and lived with them? Not many children could say that.

Hadn't Lucretia Ann been wearing really, truly Indian garments, even though they were so filthy that clean Mrs. Prence had removed them with disgust? What other little girl had done that?

Hadn't they stolen away at midnight into a black, lonely desert? Wasn't that brave?

Indeed they had done all these things, but they forgot that the whole adventure which had brought such deep suffering upon dozens of people was caused by their disobedience and heedlessness.

In fact, by morning they both seemed so pleased with themselves that Mr. Prence called them aside to try and impress upon them the seriousness of the adventure. And Dimmis found out something which Lucretia Ann herself hardly knew. Gentle Mr. Prence could scold, and scold hard! He pointed out the terrible worry, the delay, the sorrow, and troubles that had been caused by the children. He said in part:

"You girls were disobedient; you were heedless and naughty. You had been told repeatedly to keep always on the trail. We had explained why you should do so. You did not mind. You rushed away after your cat, and frolicked for hours beside the river.

"Now, Lucretia Ann, listen to me. Dimmis' parents can deal with her as they think best. But as for you—*you are to stay in or by our own wagons all the rest of the trip.* No wandering about camp, no riding in other folks' wagons or eating other folks' meals."

Lucretia Ann stared at Dimmis with wide blue eyes, and Dimmis looked back with astonished black ones. No more jolly rides together?

"Futhermore," Father continued his lecture, *"Benjamin is to stay in his cage all of the time.* If he gets out and tries to run away, let him run. You are not to leave the road by so much as an inch to hunt for him. And if he goes, do not let me hear one whimper out of you. That miserable cat (Lucretia Ann hugged Benjamin until he howled as Father said that) has caused more trouble than I care to think of, and has upset the convenience of dozens of people. We should have realized the folly of bringing him. From first to last he has been a nuisance.

"I doubt if your mother and I recover from the effects of the suspense for weeks, and as for Dimmis' parents—well, they had to endure it a day longer. Do you understand what I have said?"

Father walked away. His talk put an end to all their heroic, princesslike feelings. Both were quiet for a few minutes.

"Well," Dimmis finally said with her lips trembling, "I did not know your father could scold like that."

"He can, but he doesn't do it very often. And the worst of it is we deserve it. Do you see how white and sick my father and mother look? And yours must look the same." At the mention of her parents Dimmis began to cry and Lucretia Ann joined her. Both girls finally wiped their eyes, and resolved then and there to be so very good that a small halo would follow that part of the caravan where they were on the rest of the trail.

The day's journey now began. Benjamin was put into his cage, which was fastened onto the back of the light spring wagon where Lucretia Ann and Dimmis were riding on the bedding. They could lean over and talk to the cat as the wagon jogged along.

"Benjamin, kitty," said Lucretia Ann coaxingly, "did you listen when Father was talking about you? Father meant every word he said, and he never, never breaks his word. So you will be good, will you not? He says if you run away he'll leave you all alone. This is a dreadful, awful place to be by one's self, with coyotes and Indians and big, black deserts at night. Don't you remember how that owl hooted and everything seemed to be chasing us? You will be good, won't you, kitty darling?"

227

"Kitty darling" gave a solemn wink. He nodded his head, cocked it to one side, and seemed to smile.

"He says he'll mind, Lucretia Ann," said Dimmis excitedly. "He knows what you are saying, and he means to be good. Wasn't that cunning?"

"He's such a nice cat," agreed Lucretia Ann.

And yet, after all that, Benjamin broke his promise. Broke it right in two. That very noon! Think of it!

When they stopped for lunch, Tom unlatched the cage to feed the cat. Someone jogged his arm, the door flew open, and Benjamin with a leap was out of the cage, leaving a long, red scratch on Tom's arm. The cat had learned to hate his prison, and now he was off into the sage wishing for a merry chase, for the cage was the worst punishment he could endure. He looked back over his shoulder as if to say:

"Come on, Lucretia Ann, I'll beat you in a race. It's time for another frolic."

"O Benjamin, stop, stop," wailed Lucretia Ann. "Tom, run as fast as your heels can carry you, for Father says we may not chase him, and he'll be forever lost. O Tom, run!"

"Run! Run! Run!" echoed Dimmis.

"I'll catch him, don't worry," called Tom, but just then Father, who had seen nothing of what was going on said: "Tom, come on over here and help water the horses. We must be on our way at once."

"I must go, but maybe I can get him later," said Tom.

The two small girls stood at the edge of the road, wringing their hands and calling sadly for Benjamin, who paid no more attention to them than to the rattling of the dry leaves in the sage-brush. He was having one of his beautiful frol-ics, and saw no reason why it should be stopped.

The bugle sounded. With a stifled sob Lucretia Ann jumped into the wagon, followed by the weeping Dimmis.

"Be still, and do not let anyone see us cry," whispered Lucretia Ann. "Father said we must not even whimper, and we have caused plenty of trouble already."

They looked hopefully at the spot where Ben-jamin had vanished until it was hidden by a turn in the trail. Tom came riding up with a word of comfort and said cheerily:

"I have to ride behind with the cattle. And I will keep a sharp lookout, and tell all the fellows to do so. We will surely find your cat, Sister Ann."

But though Thomas lagged behind much long-er than was wise, and though he circled in and out among the brush no mischievous little cat came whisking out from among the shadows to meet him.

Benjamin was not to be found. He was again lost.

The next two days were among the hardest part of the trip for Lucretia Ann and Dimmis. Both were tired and half ill from the effects of their recent experience. Dimmis wanted her mother and father and that precious baby Faith. Lucretia Ann missed her cat, and thought of a thousand unhappy things which might have happened to the poor little fellow. When Father found out that same night that Benjamin was gone, he was truly sorry, for he too was fond of the mischievous kitten. But being sorry did not seem to call him from that lonely, dark desert.

It was indeed good to reach the trading post, and to settle down and live like civilized folks, even though you lived only in some tents and some wagons. It was good to have new, fresh food, and to run in and out of the huge stockades, dressed in clean, starchy clothes, and watch the colorful cowboys and plainsmen, the scouts, the soldiers, the other caravaners, and the Indians. It was good to meet Brother Stephen again, and to be a part of this gay, exciting life.

Lucretia Ann did not forget Benjamin. Not that dear little cat! Whenever a string of wagons, or even a stray horseman pulled in, the child would walk up with her friendly manner and say hopefully:

"You didn't see a beautiful tortoise-shell cat walking all alone down the trail, did you?"

But much as everyone longed to please Lucretia Ann, nobody had seen a beautiful tortoise-shell cat walking all alone down the trail.

So there was nothing to think but that Benjamin was living alone in the sagebrush with the whirring grasshoppers, the lively little grey liz-

ards, the horned owls, and the scurrying jack rabbits.

Sometimes Lucretia Ann went off by herself and cried a little cry for the faithful companion, and she would say:

"I know just exactly how my poor mother felt when she lost me."

But too much was happening for many lonely minutes, and the days flew by until towards evening of the third day the long caravan, of which the Greensleave family were members, drew in. When you have thought that you might never see your precious little daughter again, it is a joyful thing to clasp her to your heart, and the whole Greensleave family, and the rest of the caravan, clung to Dimmis and Lucretia Ann as though they could never again let them out of their sight.

"Lucretia Ann," said Dimmis, happily, "we thought your father was cross when he said you must stay by your own wagons and your own mother the rest of the journey, but now that I see my mother I don't ever want to get an inch away from her. Not an inch."

"Well, I don't care either, if I do have to stay with our wagons, if I can have little Faith with me some of the time. She's just as glad to see me as she is to see you. Aren't you, Faithie?"

"You shall have her whenever you want," said

Mrs. Greensleave. "She has missed you very much."

"I thought maybe you would bring Benjamin. You didn't see my poor little tortoise-shell cat walking alone down the trail, did you?" asked Lucretia Ann of the party. But *they* had not seen a poor, lonely little cat.

And now the caravan was preparing to leave. Father, with his faithful little shadow, Lucretia Ann, at his side was in the trading post doing some last shopping. Lucretia Ann was delightedly fingering a pile of bright calicos which had been just unwrapped, and had been chosen to catch the eyes of the Indians. There were gaudy reds, greens, flaming oranges and purples like the most blazing prairie sunsets. At the bottom of the pile Lucretia Ann found a plain piece of turkey-red calico.

"Oh, here is some cloth just like my lovely birthday dress," she said to herself. "My, I get so mad when I think of that dirty Dark Fawn running around in it. If I hadn't been such a bad girl I should ask Father to buy material for another, but I do not dare. He thinks losing that and my shoes was a just punishment for not minding."

While she was fingering the bright pieces, a

heavy hand was placed on her shoulder and she heard a guttural voice saying:

"Keeshan, Keeshan."

"That's my Indian grandmother," thought Lucretia Ann, "that's just the way she tried to say my name."

Quick as a flash she whirled about, and flung her arms about the wrinkled squaw who had been so kind to her.

"Father," she called, "come and see the nice Indian who was so good to me."

Father came and shook the kindly old woman's hand again and again. But she did not seem at ease. She spoke quickly to a tall Indian who was standing near, and he went outside, returning in a few moments with a half-breed, who talked both the English and the Indian language, and who could tell the story the grandmother wanted known.

The Indians had not meant to steal the children, he said. Indeed, they had not wanted them at all. They were returning from a huckleberry expedition and wanted to go right on across the valley, to trade with a friendly tribe.

They had found the children who had been left behind, and a few of them had decided to stay and take a short cut across the prairie, by which they hoped to overtake the parents in several hours at the most. They would undoubtedly have done so, save for the storm which brought such confusion, and which covered all tracks so faithfully. The Indians had judged that the party was far ahead of them, when they failed to see dust from the rear. They could not know that part of the caravan had camped below the hill several miles distant, and that the remainder had returned to the river. So the Indians, after much parley decided to push on as rapidly as possible, thinking to overtake either the caravan where the children belonged or another which would take charge of them. When night came on, with no sign of any whites, they decided to camp and wait until some caravan came along.

Now it happened that a large wagon train had departed a day before the Prence party started, and as we have seen, caravaners who came to the river when the children were lost stayed to help hunt. That was why practically no one passed during the two days the Indians waited.

When the children stole away the Indians were sleeping soundly. They were awakened by the passing of the Prence caravan, and judged that the girls had heard it, and had run to join it. So the Indians decided to fish two days longer, before rejoining their party. But the grandmother was uneasy, and when several Indians who had come on them at the river (among whom was the grandson, the tall, young Indian), had announced that they were going to travel on to the post the grandmother had decided to join them. She was so happy to know that the white papooses were safe, and hoped that the white father would know that she had tried to care for them.

Father shook her hand and thanked her again and again through the interpreter. Then he said to Lucretia Ann:

"We must make her a present, Daughter. What do you think she would like?"

"A dress, Father, I am sure, for all these Indian women seem to like this bright calico so much. I know the grandmother would like a bright, pretty dress, and I should like to have her clean."

The grandmother did want a dress. In fact, she wanted all the patterns. She and Lucretia Ann and the squaws who were standing by had a hard time deciding, but finally a glowing scarlet with bright flowers running through it satisfied her. To this Mr. Prence added a piece of bacon, and a sack of flour, and the grandmother's wrinkled face was wreathed with smiles as she grunted again and again to express her thanks.

Then Father, through the interpreter, told of how the children had slipped away at midnight and followed the trail in the dark. The grandmother's face looked so sorry, and in her eyes shone the gentle light that had made Lucretia Ann think of Grandmother Pettigrew. When father finished his tale, the grandmother grew animated, and grasped Lucretia Ann's arm, speaking as fast as she could talk, as though she personally wanted to tell the child something.

"She has a present for the white child at her tepee. She wants her to come there," was explained.

"Where it is?" asked Father. "We are getting packed up for an early morning's start."

"Just over the hill—perhaps half a mile."

"Shall we go?" inquired Lucretia Ann eagerly.

"I think we might as well. It will take but a few minutes."

"Then let us get Tom and Stephen. They would like to see this Indian grandmother. They

237

would like to see her tepee, too. I wish they would have some of those big fish there. Tom thinks I'm fibbing when I tell of them. Maybe my mother and Dimmis would like to come with us."

Right where the sun set became the home of Lucretia Ann and her tortoise-shell cat, who, though born to trouble as the sparks fly upwards, had managed somehow to come safely across the Oregon Trail.

CHAPTER FIFTEEN

MOTHER was having a gala time ironing, and had no time for gallivanting around the country, she said. There was a big basket of clothes sprinkled down, and she and some of the other women were heating irons in an immense Dutch oven. Thinking this might be the last chance to indulge in this luxury for some weeks, they were piling chests and boxes with freshly ironed clothing. Dimmis was away with her father, but the boys gladly jumped at the chance.

The grandmother had gone on ahead, leaving her grandson and the interpreter to guide the party to her tepee. They neared a small Indian encampment, and went toward a large wickiup, or tepee, a little apart from the rest. Then it seemed as though Lucretia Ann had gone wild. She gave a scream and darted ahead as though wings were on her heavy shoes. *No wonder she ran, and ran fast!*

Sitting majestically in front of the tepee was Benjamin, carefully washing his face. And all the time Lucretia Ann had supposed him to be miles and miles away on the desert playing with the lizards and the jackrabbits. The clever grandmother had tied a buckskin thong to a tree, and fastened the other end to a leather collar about his neck, to keep him from running away.

Lucretia Ann reached her pet. She hugged, kissed, and cried over him, while the grandmother, who had found Benjamin on the lonely trail, stood in the doorway of the tepee and looked on with smiling eyes. In her hand was an exquisitely woven basket, which she handed to Lucretia Ann.

"The grandmother is giving me one of her lovely baskets to remember her by. Isn't that nice?" she cried to her father. Then she lifted the lid, and gave a still greater cry of delight.

There lay the red-topped morocco shoes!

Dark Fawn, who could not wear them, had laid them aside, and the squaw had picked them up and hidden them, thinking that chance might allow her to return them someday to the white child to whom she had taken such a fancy.

"My pretty shoes! My pretty shoes! And my kitty. Aren't we all happy together, Father?" she exclaimed.

As for the birthday dress, Lucretia Ann never saw it again. At first, when she thought of the pretty scarlet thing upon which Grandmother Pettigrew had put literally thousands of stitches, she wrinkled up that delightfully sunny little face into a dreadful scowl, clenched her fists, and shook them in the face of an invisible dark-skinned child who was running about in the garment which was probably stiff with grease and dirt.

But as time rolled by, the beaded buckskin tunic, nicely cleaned, became one of the child's most cherished treasures. She loved to put it on, and dance and strut about while she bragged about the time when she had lived with the Indians.

And now the story of little Miss Lucretia Ann Prence and her tortoise-shell cat who crossed over the Oregon Trail is about finished. There were many adventures still, and the happenings of each

day would make a story. But for the remainder of the trip a better little girl and a better little cat would have been hard to find.

Benjamin stayed in his cage and was as good as any frolicsome cat could possibly be. It's hard to be shut in a dusty, stuffy cage, when you want to be romping over the desert. But it's nice to be good, even if you have to, isn't it?

Lucretia Ann stayed by her own wagons, which was no hardship for her. The children always flocked about her, like bees about a drop of honey, so when she could not go and play with them, they all sought her out. So perhaps it was poor Mrs. Prence who was punished, especially on rainy days, when they all wanted to crowd into her immaculate wagons. But if she grew impatient she thought of those dismal nights when she waited around the huge signal bonfires, peering desperately into the dark shadows and wondering if she would ever see her baby again. Dimmis, too, had to stay in or by her own wagons, but there was always company for her, also.

So they went on, and on—and on—

There were steep hills to climb and deep rivers to cross. Several times the wagons had to be unpacked, calked with tar, and used for rafts. Once, they had to be let down with ropes from steep, high cliffs, and each traveler who climbed down had a rope about his waist for safety.

There were Indian alarms. Lucretia Ann knew what it was to lie inside the circle of wagons, with each man standing ready with his weapon, and thinking that at any moment the terrible war whoop of Indians would be heard. Once a band of several hundred warriors in war paint and gorgeous trappings passed the caravans without looking to the right or to the left. They were on their way to fight a neighboring tribe, but the fright their passing brought was very real.

Sometimes the fiercest winds blew. Once the ground was white with snow. Again, there were Italian skies, beautiful weather, and happy days when all were filled with peace and hope as they thought how near they were to the new land.

The last week it rained so that it seemed as though giants with huge buckets were pouring floods of water through the clouds. Sometimes it got so dull that Lucretia Ann would put on her little waterproof cape with the gathered hood, and tramp miles beside her father. Once she said, looking like a little drowned rat:

"Why couldn't God have sent us part of this rain when we needed it so badly in the desert?"

One day the clouds lifted at mid-afternoon, and sent dazzling, warm October sunshine over the land. It showed four horseback riders coming up over a little ridge, and outlined them for a moment as though they had been a group of statuary. Was this the forerunner of another Indian fright? Mr. Prence hastily raised his spy glasses. No, he was sure they were whites. They came nearer and nearer. Then a shout was raised.

"It's the Sears boys, and Perry and John Lothrop. It's our neighbors from Vermont!"

The journey was over. The friends had ridden ahead to guide the caravan to their new home over the hill. Just before the sun was setting the whole caravan reached the crest of the hill. For miles below them was spread out the valley which was to be their home for years to come.

Lucretia Ann grabbed Benjamin from his cage.

"I want him to see his new home with the others," she cried excitedly.

They both looked. Over across the valley the sun was setting. It was sinking beneath a grove of tall poplars.

"Benjamin," said Lucretia Ann softly, "right where the sun is, that's where I want our new home. And listen, kitty, I'm so happy I can hardly wait. Nobody knows it, and you are the only one I am telling, for it's a secret. But I shall burst if I do not tell someone. If we like it here, and get a home built, our Grandmother Pettigrew is coming too. Uncle Peter says she may, and he always has his way. She told me because I can keep a secret, and you can too, can't you, Kitty Benjamin?"

Kitty Benjamin cocked his head on one side. He gave a long "meow" and licked Lucretia Ann's hand.

The sun sank from sight. And the spot where it vanished did in time become the home of Lucretia Ann Prence and her tortoise-shell cat who, though born to trouble as the sparks fly upwards, had managed somehow to come safely across the trail.

THANK YOU

THE story of the adventures of LUCRETIA ANN ON THE OREGON TRAIL is purely fictitious, yet the author has endeavored to make the setting and background of the story authentic. To this end she has delved into western history and extends a "thank you" to the pioneer pages of *The Idaho Daily Statesman,* to the old-timers whom she has interviewed, and to the Pocahontas Chapter D.A.R., whose Idaho programs first interested her in The Old Oregon Trail and the history of our state. Among books read for the setting and background of the story are the following:

Oregon Trail - - - - - - - - - - - PARKMAN
History of Idaho - - - - - - - - - - BROSNAN
History of Idaho - - - - - - - - - - FRENCH
History of Idaho - - - - - - - - McCONNELL
Whitman's Ride Through Savage Lands - - - NIXON
Red Heroines of the Northwest - - - - DEFENBACH
We Must March - - - - - - - - - - MORROW
On To Oregon - - - - - - - - - - MORROW
Narcissa Whitman - - - - - - - - - CANNON
Fifteen Thousand Miles by Stage - - - - STRAHORN
Reminiscences of the Oregon Trail - - - - FULTON
Reminiscences - - - - - - - - - - - WRIGHT
The Astorians - - - - - - - WASHINGTON IRVING
Captain Bonneville - - - - - WASHINGTON IRVING
Reminiscences - - - - - - - - - - GOULDER